P9-EEU-148

DRAGONS VS. DRONES

razOr
bill

An Imprint of Penguin Random House

An Imprint of Penguin Random House

Penguin.com

Copyright © 2016 Penguin Random House LLC

Penguin Random House supports copyright. Copyright fuels creativity, encourages diverse voices, promotes free speech, and creates a vibrant culture. Thank you for buying an authorized edition of this book and for complying with copyright laws by not reproducing, scanning, or distributing any part of it in any form without permission. You are supporting writers and allowing Penguin Random House to continue to publish books for every reader.

ISBN: 978-1-59514-797-4

Printed in the United States of America

1 3 5 7 9 10 8 6 4 2

Book design by Anthony Elder

This is a work of fiction. Names, characters, places, and incidents either are the product of the author's imagination or are used fictitiously, and any resemblance to actual persons, living or dead, businesses, companies, events, or locales is entirely coincidental.

To Rick Niedziela
Who showed us what real courage looks like

Chapter 1

The air was nothing but smoke and ash, lingering over the room and covering everything in darkness. Forms moved in the haze like shapeless wraiths or spirits of the dead. When the iron-forged front door opened—which it rarely did—sunlight tentatively entered the room and fell upon the endless rows of swords and spears that lined the blackened walls, just waiting for blood. In short, Wilhelm's Forge was a grim, fire-blasted hole—tucked onto the side of a bustling city street and ignored by the most sensible folk.

But for Driele Reiter, it was one of the few places in Dracone where she felt like she belonged, and more importantly, where she could hide away from the crowds and be alone with her work. Dree was twelve but looked older: tall and lean, with arms as hard as the beaten steel that they formed. Sweat dripped freely down from her forehead and created rivulets on her soot-stained cheeks like fresh rain snaking its way through the dirt.

Dree was a welder's apprentice and had been for almost two years. It was trying work, but it also was a rare chance to design and build and think about something other than the memories—grainy images of moments she wanted to forget, or brilliant flashes of scarlet and smoke. She stood over the blazing hot forge, lovingly pulling her afternoon's work out of the fire with a set of iron tongs and heavy leather gloves. She had already welded most of the contraption together with a torch, but she always liked to drop her creations in the fire at the end to smooth the sides into near-glass. It was the little details she admired.

Dree and the other apprentice made many things in the busy metal shop: broadswords, tools, even gleaming, fire-resistant armor. But a few months ago, Dree had received a different assignment from her boss, the domineering Master Wilhelm, and one that she particularly loved: a toy. She had worked on it every free moment she had, when the swords and shields were done and she could return to her special project.

It was a magnificent thing—a black iron dragonfly, each piece meticulously forged from casts of her own creation and then welded into place with a small torch. It was more intricate than anything she had ever made before, with almost ethereal quad wings, bulbous eyes, and delicate legs that the master himself would have struggled to make. After dumping cold water on the toy and eliciting a shower of steam, Dree carefully picked it up, smiling for the first time that day. She wore gloves, but she didn't need them. Heat had never bothered Dree. In fact, even when the hottest fire danced over her calloused, leather-hard hands, it barely seemed to touch her. It had been that way her entire life.

And look what that's done for you, she thought bitterly, fighting off a sudden image that flashed into her mind like a fork of lightning. Smoke and ash, but not in a welder's shop—the smell of burning furniture and wood and flesh. The screaming she still heard at night. And worst of all, a little boy who never left the fire.

Dree shook her head, trying to get back to the present. She had created something beautiful, and she could allow herself some time to enjoy it before it was sold off to some rich, young Draconian for more than Dree made in a week. Maybe a month.

"Finally done?" Sasha—Wilhelm's other apprentice—asked scornfully.

He looked like a welder's apprentice: tall and strong with broad shoulders and a matching block chin. Dree didn't like to admit it, but he was handsome—the heat seemed to have carved his face into stone, proud and rigid, while his eyes were a warm almond brown that moved from friendly to condescending almost instantly.

Sasha had no love for toys. He wanted only to forge swords and spears and talk about how he would much rather be sticking them into a dragon's black heart up in the mountains. It was one of the many things Dree and Sasha didn't agree on.

"Perfection takes time," Dree responded quietly, running her fingers over the lattice wings. Despite Sasha's comment, even Master Wilhelm would appreciate this.

"And a toy is a perfect waste of time," Sasha retorted, shutting down his forge.

It was getting late, and the shop was closing for the day. Wilhelm would be in to inspect their work shortly—usually to bluster and curse and complain about his apprentices.

Dree ignored Sasha. She was the better welder by far, but Sasha was the clear favorite. Wilhelm said it himself all the time. It wasn't about their performance—Dree just had an unfortunate habit of getting into trouble.

Of course, Sasha had no idea just how intricate the dragonfly really was. The inside was filled with countless tiny mechanisms of Dree's own creation: gears and pistons and other things Sasha—and Master Wilhelm—couldn't even begin to fathom.

Dree thought of how her father would react if he knew she was creating such things. He would be furious. He didn't want Dree doing anything out of the ordinary and attracting attention to herself. Her father was a brilliant man who was afraid to be brilliant. He was afraid of a lot of things, actually. You wouldn't know it to look at him: He had Dree's wild chestnut hair and piercing blue eyes, and he was lined with the shadows of muscles that had long since faded after too many years spent in an armchair. He'd hurt his back many years ago, bad enough that he couldn't lift anything or even really bend. In fact, Abelard wasn't able to work at all, and it was up to Dree's mother to keep the house afloat. With five kids, that wasn't easy.

Dree had left school at ten to get a job and help out her mother. She remembered the day well. She'd barely managed to pull the huge cast-iron door open before sneaking inside, her tiny hands trembling at her stomach.

She needed a job . . . now.

Master Wilhelm appeared over her, eyes as dark as coal. He was a welder to the core—a belly like a keg and a much-singed salt-and-pepper beard.

"What do you want, girl?" he asked, scanning over her ratty peasant's clothes.

"I want a job," she murmured, unable to meet his hard gaze. "I can weld."

He guffawed, his belly shaking like her mother's holiday pudding. "Are you mad?" he asked. "You look like a starving dormouse."

Dree stiffened. "I can weld."

Master Wilhelm stared at her, a hammer slung over his shoulder. "Is that so?"

"I know fire," she said quietly. "Give me a torch."

He paused for a long moment, and finally he shrugged and gestured to the forge.

"I haven't had a good laugh in a while," he sneered. "Make me something."

He had returned to his work, still laughing, as Dree slipped on an overlarge apron and gloves, tied back her tangled hair, and started. Dree had never welded a day in her life, but when she'd set out for a job that morning, she knew she should play to her strengths. She liked to build, and she was born with fire. It was an hour later when she showed him her work. Wilhelm turned from his forge, sweat pouring from his scowling visage.

His eyes widened.

In Dree's slender hands sat an exact replica of the palace, welded from scraps and yet perfect in its details. A flag stood on the highest peak, the metal welded paper-thin and bent as if blowing in the northern wind.

He stared at it for a long moment, not speaking. Then he turned back to his work.

"You can start tomorrow."

Two years later, Dree was still working at the forge. Of course, Wilhelm liked to remind her that a forge was "no place for a girl," as he had said constantly in those first few days. But Dree had proven her worth a thousand times over—creating shields smoother than the surface of the morning lake that bordered the city and intricate metalwork like locks, scales, and trinkets that Sasha could never hope to replicate—and so far Wilhelm had never had a reason to fire her. She just had to keep it that way.

But neither Master Wilhelm nor Dree's father was there at the moment, and she simply couldn't resist showing Sasha exactly what a *toy* could do. Making sure her back was completely blocking Sasha's view, Dree softly put her hand to the top of the iron-forged toy, where a little metal shaft led straight to the heart of the dragonfly—the engine. It just needed a bit of fuel to operate. A bit of fire. Luckily for Dree, the fire was always there.

She just had to let it out.

Dree's hand rippled with delicate red and blue flames, which should have burned her skin but instead passed over it like warm water. The dancing fire raced into the dragon-fly's heart, and suddenly brilliant light shone from the many openings in the black iron, as if a lantern had been lit inside. Dree grinned wolfishly as the fire grew brighter.

It was working.

The lattice wings suddenly beat frantically, as if alive, and then picked up speed, moving in a blur. It shouldn't have been possible—even Dree knew that. But dragons could fly, borne by fire, and just as she had guessed, so could steel and iron.

The toy dragonfly lifted off the table, its quad wings almost humming, and then it tilted forward, buzzing across the forge and heading straight for Sasha, who finally realized what was going on.

"What the—" he managed, ducking as the dragonfly raced over his head.

He looked at Dree incredulously.

"How did you do that?"

Dree shrugged. "Like I said, perfection takes time."

She so enjoyed the look on Sasha's face. It was well worth the risk.

And then Master Wilhelm raced into the shop, panicked.

"Clean up," he barked, rushing over to a scattered pile of weaponry. "I heard that the Prime Minister is going to pop in." He stopped when he saw his apprentices just standing there, confused. "Here!" he blustered, spittle flying from his mouth. "Move!"

Dree had just started for the toy dragonfly, which was buzzing around the far end of the shop, when the front door swung open, allowing sunlight to flood the windowless forge once again. The smiling Prime Minister strolled in, flanked by two of his cabinet members, who were eyeing the forge with obvious distaste. They all looked impeccable as usual. Francis Xidorne was the shining symbol of the new Dracone—smart and cultured and trendy.

His famous raven hair was long and curly, falling almost to his eyes. He wasn't a tall man, but his gleaming black boots and their generous four-inch heels gave him more height and matched the half cape he sometimes sported. Even at forty-nine, only a few wrinkles lined the corners of his oft-smiling lips. While he didn't wear the fire-resistant armor that was so popular among the younger generation, he did have a silver necklace with a lone dragon fang dangling around his neck, a sign of the thriving market of dragon paraphernalia and the larger trend of killing dragons in general. Dree despised dragon hunters, but she wasn't about to tell Francis Xidorne that.

"Welcome to my humble shop." Master Wilhelm hurried over with a massive hand outstretched. "My apologies for the state of it—"

"Nonsense," Francis said. "That's the point of these visits: to see how our city is bustling." He looked around, flashing his sparkling white teeth—whiter than any Dree had ever seen. "And it looks like business is good."

Master Wilhelm was ecstatic. He loved the Prime Minister and was always going on about how he had turned Dracone around when he ordered that the dragons be hunted to the point of extinction and the path cleared for economic and cultural growth. It was that economic growth that had left Dree's father behind, along with all the old Draconian families—the ones who had admired the dragons, the ones who had counted them as friends.

"Yes, very good," Master Wilhelm said, nodding and gesturing around the shop. "Orders have been pouring in, especially for weapons for our soldiers and the dragon hunters in the mountains. Excellent business, that. Never mind tools for building roads and houses and . . . Dree, come here and show the Prime Minister the toy you were working on today. Toys, if you can imagine! That's how you know times are good."

Dree froze, watching the dragonfly out of the corner of her eye. This was not good. Francis smiled at Dree expectantly, while his two cabinet members just looked bored, whispering to each other and checking their gold-plated pocket watches.

"Will you come over here?" Wilhelm asked again, his voice lower.

Dree shuffled over, desperately trying to think of an excuse not to show Francis her toy. Sasha looked at her with a raised eyebrow. Toys weren't supposed to fly around like that. Even the dim-witted Sasha knew something was wrong.

"Well?" Master Wilhelm asked, sounding more and more agitated.

Dree had no choice. She had to show them. She turned to where the dragonfly had been circling in the corner and stifled a curse. It was gone. Dree looked around wildly and then noticed in horror that the dragonfly was now hovering directly over Francis's curly black head. Master Wilhelm's eyes went wide when he saw it, and he looked between the dragonfly and Dree, horrified.

"How?" he said.

Dree was just going to retrieve the toy when the glowing fire in the dragonfly's heart suddenly flickered and went out. It dropped out of the sky, thudded loudly off of Francis's head, and smashed into the ground. One of the beautiful latticework wings snapped off, and Dree forlornly watched it skid across the stone floor of the shop.

Francis gasped and grabbed his head, wincing as blood flowed through his manicured fingers. The two cabinet members rushed to help him, throwing Wilhelm dirty looks, and then all three men quickly exited the shop, with Francis managing one last forced smile and a "thank you for your contribution to Dracone" before disappearing through the door. Master Wilhelm turned on Dree, his clenched fists shaking like leaves.

"Out," he whispered.

Dree frowned. She had expected yelling and screaming and maybe at least a mention of the fact that her toy was just *flying*, but not this. He couldn't mean it.

"I'm sorry—" she said.

He pointed to the front door, his whole body trembling with rage. Dree had embarrassed him in front of his hero. She had never seen him so livid.

"Get out," he said. "And don't come back."

Dree felt her stomach drop into her boots. "You're firing me?"

"That's right," he snarled. "Leave the gloves and apron and get out of my shop."

She snuck a glance at Sasha, who at least looked a little sympathetic, and then slowly put her gloves and apron on the closest table. What was her father going to say? They didn't have much money as it was, and the family depended on her weekly wage from the forge. How were they going to get by now? Her mother would be absolutely furious—she'd have to work even longer hours at the steel mill.

Dree grabbed her old leather pack and shuffled toward the exit, trying not to meet Wilhelm's eyes. She'd worked dutifully in his shop for two years, and he was just throwing her out like a beggar at the door. She couldn't believe it.

"Take the bug," he growled.

Dree tenderly picked up the broken dragonfly and its

wing, tucking them into her pack, and then heaved the door open, stepping out into the fading sunlight. It was a beautiful, clear evening, and the streets of Dracone were as packed and chaotic as ever.

The door slammed shut behind her with a last fiery gust of smoke, the smell wafting over her nostrils.

The city had many pungent scents of its own. It was a world in transition: Half-constructed buildings stretched toward the azure sky, bordered by shops and houses that were as old as the dirt they were standing on. Metal and wood joined together haphazardly in horse-drawn carts, while towering brick smokestacks spewed black clouds into the air. Dree stepped around a stray dog darting along the cobblestone street, chased away by raucous merchants selling beef and potatoes alongside dragon fangs and scales and hearts. Rich, young Draconians stood there, matching white fangs to fire-resistant armor they'd never use, all with scorched-off eyebrows, elaborate painted designs on their faces, and half-shaven heads.

Dree thought it was all garish and bizarre, but that was the new Dracone.

She looked across the sprawling city, to where her house was nestled in a maze of overcrowded dockside shacks overlooking the lake. That was where her father and three younger siblings were waiting. She pictured Abi's face. She had let her sister down too.

Dree suddenly turned the other way, toward the towering wall of mountains to the east. There was no way she was going home right now, she decided, pushing through the crowd toward the outskirts of the city, her eyes locked on one snowcapped mountain in particular, where a hidden cave sat perched on the slopes. She needed some time to think of a story to tell her parents about why she'd been fired.

And more importantly, there was someone she needed to see.

Chapter 2

Marcus felt something bounce off the back of his head. He sighed deeply. Judging from the relative size and weight of the object, he suspected it was an eraser, which meant Justin and Ian were throwing things at each other from across the back of the classroom as usual. He heard muted snickers, but that was probably more of a "fortunate coincidence" kind of laugh than the result of a deliberate attempt. He hoped, anyway.

Marcus wasn't generally the target of any bullying, but he wasn't the kind of guy they would apologize to either. He was stuck somewhere in between popular and completely invisible, which was fine by him. Actually, fully invisible would have been great too—he'd had more than enough attention growing up.

When you were part of the most inexplicable disappearance in state history, you learned to live with questions and cameras and closed curtains. Marcus had even learned to live with the constant stares and the laughter and the older kids pushing him into walls and lockers. But Marcus had never learned to live with the names they had for his father: spy, turncoat . . . traitor.

Students had spat the names at him as he walked down the hallway, and while the teachers of course didn't say anything, even they looked at him like he was a product of something corrupt and contagious. Eventually his uncle Jack—a close friend of his father's who had taken over custody of Marcus—had moved Marcus across Arlington to a new school for a fresh start. He had been able to slip into relative obscurity here, and Marcus liked it that way. He could continue his research in private.

Brian, Marcus's best friend, glanced over and smirked. He was slightly more popular than Marcus—though that wasn't really saying much—because he played football, which his dad insisted on despite Brian's strong preference for video games. His sandy blond hair was always artfully messed up, which wasn't fooling anyone, and he had a strong fondness for monochrome golf shirts. Brian was on an unending quest for total popularity, but he was held back by the fact that he was a little chunky and had a bit of an ongoing acne issue. Not to mention he—like Marcus—was completely useless with girls. Brian usually got hives whenever he was near a girl, and Marcus never got close enough to any to find out how he'd react.

Their high-strung math teacher, Mrs. Saunders, was droning on in the background about multiplication tables, while Marcus lazily stared out the window, barely hearing a thing. He knew all that stuff anyway: Math and science were definitely his strong suits. He was a three-time winner of the State Physics Bowl and had won the Math Bowl twice. In the last Physics Bowl, he had presented a quantifiable theory to explain the spatial distortions in a wormhole—the second-place participant had built an electric conductor. Needless to say, it was a short deliberation. Most of the judges didn't even fully comprehend Marcus's theory—they just knew that it was well beyond anything they understood. He got a ribbon.

Too bad that didn't impress girls. If Marcus could catch a football, maybe they would talk to him. But considering he had string bean arms and the general athleticism of an armchair, he doubted that was going to happen anytime soon. Not that it mattered.

He had more important things to worry about.

Marcus gazed out the window at the ominous tide of storm clouds approaching on the horizon, bubbling and bursting with electrostatic power as they swept across the sky. The October air was warm and muggy, even in the air-conditioned classroom, and he knew that they would probably get a heavy shower in the next hour or two.

But will it actually be a full thunderstorm? Will it happen again?

Today was the first of the month . . . the end of the line. If *it* happened, he would finally know.

Marcus fiddled with the old watch on his wrist, the faded gold polish revealing dark chrome beneath. It didn't even work—it hadn't in almost five years. But Marcus still wore it every day as a reminder. He stared at it thoughtfully, wondering as always why his father had left it behind. He'd only ever taken it off once in Marcus's entire life.

The night he left.

Marcus was just turning back to the front of the class when he accidentally met eyes with Lori Tarmen, a quiet brunette whose style fell somewhere between emo and hipster, and who had been in Marcus's class every year since he'd gotten to his new school. Her eyes were big and dark and framed with the longest eyelashes he had ever seen, and Marcus felt himself flush with embarrassment. He quickly turned away again.

But when Marcus snuck another glance a minute later, she was wearing a wry smile, keeping her eyes locked on the board. Marcus wondered if Lori knew about his dad—about the yearlong investigation and the allegations and the label that Marcus was stuck with for life: a traitor's son.

His arms started to prickle, the hairs rising, and he felt an intense heat pressing on his skin from the inside out. He knew he needed to calm down . . . and fast. But the anger and resentment were always there, waiting to erupt. *Traitor. Deserter.*

They were all liars.

"She definitely has a thing for you," Brian whispered.

Marcus rolled his eyes. "How did you even see that?"

"I see everything."

Mrs. Saunders glanced back from the chalkboard, and they both fell silent just long enough for her to return to her notes. Three people were actually copying them.

"I'm sure she's just being nice," Marcus said.

He doubted any girl would have a crush on him—especially a girl as pretty as Lori. Girls liked football players and musicians and rebels, not gangly science geeks. And even if she did like him, Marcus could never talk to her anyway. Just the thought of talking to a girl made his stomach tighten. Better to avoid the humiliation.

Brian snorted. "Because you're so good at reading women."

"I read them fine," he replied quietly.

"You're a quitter."

"And a survivor. Now if you'll excuse me, I have daydreaming to attend to—"

The words were barely out of his mouth when an announcement came over the loudspeaker, eliciting groans and sighs as a deep voice boomed out across the classroom.

"Attention, classes." The familiar Texas drawl of Principal Fedak came through the speakers, sounding concerned. "We have just had a call from the school board, and it seems the storm today is going to be a bit . . . stronger than expected. Severe thunderstorm warnings have been posted, and so we have decided to end classes an hour early today so that everyone can get home before it hits."

The groans instantly turned to high fives and cheers. But not for Marcus. He turned back to the classroom window, his gray eyes widening.

Brian saw his intent expression and took up the groan. "Don't start."

"Teachers," Principal Fedak continued, "please ensure that all students leave in an orderly manner. Class dismissed."

So much for orderly. The class rose like a tidal wave, conversations erupting in every corner. Justin started doing a jig at the back, and Ian threw an eraser at him. But despite the uproar, Marcus was completely quiet. Another storm. And another big one. The countdown was over. Eight years . . . eight storms. But why?

Brian stood up and started packing his books, eyeing Marcus carefully.

"You're looking a bit . . . agitated again," Brian murmured.

Marcus waved a hand in dismissal and shoved everything into his backpack, already starting for the door. Students were quickly filing out as Mrs. Saunders sighed and cleaned the blackboard, her equations long forgotten. Brian scurried after him.

"Remember what we said about staying calm—"

"I am calm," Marcus snarled, jostling through the doorway.

A few weeks earlier there had been a little incident with Marcus's Xbox. He had been playing a shooter, waiting for Brian to come over and join him, when a particularly annoying online gamer had managed to kill Marcus's character yet again. By the time Brian had actually arrived, the Xbox was little more than a pile of scrap metal.

Of course, what Marcus didn't explain to Brian was that he had only smashed the Xbox up *after* to cover the fact that the entire game system had sort of caught fire and melted at the same time as Marcus's character died. He would have blamed it on a system defect or something, but he couldn't help but notice that the controller had completely melted in his hands as well . . . and he hadn't even felt it burn. That did not seem normal.

And it wasn't the first time either. Something was very wrong with Marcus, and it was getting worse. But he wasn't going to tell Brian that. He wasn't going to tell anyone.

Marcus hurried to his locker. He had to get home and check the dates. He wanted to know for sure. Snatching his beat-up skateboard out of his locker, he turned to Brian.

"I am not going to break anything," he promised.

Brian raised an eyebrow. "Fine. Vids tonight?"

"They just said there was a severe thunderstorm coming," Marcus replied, throwing his backpack over both shoulders and tightening the straps.

"Oh yeah," Brian said. "Well, we'll play it by ear."

Marcus snorted and headed outside. Brian took the bus, since he lived on the outskirts of the school district, but Marcus lived just a little too close and was stuck walking—or more often, skateboarding. It was still muggy, but a strong wind was gusting across the city now, blowing hot air that felt like it was flying straight out of the Sahara. Marcus took a worried glance at the sky. The storm clouds were coming faster now. He had to hurry home or he was going to get soaked.

He threw his skateboard out in front of him and hopped on, turning out of the parking lot and onto the adjoining sidewalk. Marcus looked like a skateboarder, though he didn't hang out with that group: his raven hair was unkempt and bordering on too long, almost reaching the top of the matching thick-rimmed glasses that sat perched on his lightly freckled nose. He had a whole closet full of faded graphic Ts and plaid button-downs, as well as jeans that were probably a bit tight, if only because he hated shopping too much to buy new ones. He also wore his favorite shoes like usual: orange-striped Adidas that were definitely due for replacing.

He was pretty good on the board by now, and he raced down the sidewalk, fixated on the brooding gray clouds that were sweeping across the sky.

Marcus was just about to turn the corner when a green sedan drove by with a familiar face staring out the window: all curling lashes and full lips and dark eyes. Marcus knew he should probably keep his own eyes on the sidewalk, but he met her gaze for just a moment, and as she drove away his skateboard rode up on the grass and abruptly stopped. Unfortunately, Marcus didn't.

He went flying, his arms flailing everywhere, and then he thudded onto the grass. His right cheek smacked against the dirt. As he watched the car drive away, Marcus hoped she hadn't seen that pathetic display. A group of seniors driving by certainly did though, all of them laughing uproariously. Marcus groaned and picked himself up. He knew girls all right—he knew they were bad news. For him, anyway.

Marcus was soon on the board again, which was a good thing because the storm was moving impossibly fast. It was already dark out, and a flash of lightning lit up the sky above him. This was going to be a particularly bad one. A haze rolled in, obscuring the Arlington skyline, and Marcus picked up his pace. He was going to get drenched.

He was just turning onto his street when a fork of lightning split the sky, momentarily breaking the haze and illuminating a tumultuous cloudscape. Marcus looked up, bracing for the rain, and then almost toppled off his skateboard again.

There was something in the clouds.

It was there for just a moment—as black as night and sharply angled like a massive bird of prey. It was gone almost immediately, but Marcus thought he saw a blazing red eye at the front, gazing downward. Marcus stared up at the swiftly moving clouds with a mixture of curiosity and alarm. What was that thing?

With a giant clap of thunder, the rain broke in a great, freezing sheet, and Marcus quickly jumped back on his board and started for home. As he rode, he felt an uncomfortable tingle moving up his spine.

Whatever that thing was, it was still watching him.

Chapter 3

As soon as she was out of the city, Dree felt her foul mood lighten. She couldn't stand to look at any more wealthy, young Draconians with their heads shaved into Mohawks or archaic symbols, dragon fangs dangling from their necks. It was almost as bad as staring at the thriving food stands knowing she couldn't afford to buy anything. Everywhere she looked, she saw her parents' disappointed faces or her younger siblings starving in the alleys. She saw failure.

But here in the rolling green hills outside of Dracone, she felt alive. There were worn cobblestone roads leading to the many smaller towns and farms that surrounded the city, but Dree quickly left those behind and cut straight through the tall grass, heading up into the hills and letting the scent of fresh pine and mountain snow wash the soot from her nostrils. Multicolored birds flitted past her, along with little yellow butterflies that rested on the tips of grass like daffodils. She smiled as she looked up at the mountain.

Her second home.

Dree climbed higher and higher, until the city was a mottled spot of brown on the plains—a sickly puddle. The gleaming palace rose from the middle of the city, seemingly untouched by the utter chaos around it. Francis would be there now, probably with a block of ice perched on his head. Dree scowled and kept moving, leaving it all behind.

Soon she was climbing a steep slope. The grass thinned and was replaced with scraggly clumps of yellowed weeds. She was sweating and happy for it—the exertion was taking her mind off of the incident at the forge. Finally, Dree pulled herself up over a rocky ledge that protruded from the mountainside. A cave was nestled there, hidden by thick brambles and by the shape of the mountain, which blocked the view from the city. It was probably the closest remaining dragon cave to the city—the last place in Dracone that the hunters were looking.

A massive figure moved in the darkness, casting an enormous shadow over Dree.

The sight would have been terrifying to most people, but not Dree. She had been to this cave hundreds of times over the years, and the shadow was a welcome sight.

A lopsided grin split her face as Lourdvang emerged from the cave, filling the entire entrance. His glistening black scales rippled and shimmered as he walked, his entire body lined with powerful muscles. Lourdvang's wings were furled closely to his back, but Dree knew that they extended some twenty feet on either side of him, like the wings of an enormous bat. He was every part a dragon: frightening and deadly. But Lourdvang's face spoke to a different past—one that humans seemed so keen to forget.

His snout held a mouth of jagged teeth, but he didn't bare them. His eyes were a brilliant blue, brighter than the lake, and they tracked Dree's expression with a warm and cunning intelligence. When he saw her, a line creased his forehead in a frown.

"You got in trouble again," he said, the words rolling off his tongue in a low, rumbling growl that was accompanied as always by a trail of black smoke.

The smoke was a trait of his particular species. Dracone was home to four different species of dragons, separated into autocratic clans by the color of their scales and the inherent abilities that went along with them.

Lourdvang was a Nightwing. Nightwings' hides were as dark as pure ebony, or shaded purple, and their personalities just and fair, though by now they mostly hated the humans who had turned against them. Once they had been close with humans and were the dragons most often used by riders like Dree's father.

There were also emerald dragons—Outliers, the wildest of the four types—which unleashed bubbling, acid-green flames that burned like molten steel, melting and incinerating anything on contact. Outliers were also the least intelligent dragon clan, and in recent years they constantly attacked humans on the outskirts of Dracone, always hunting for food . . . and for vengeance for their kin that had been killed by dragon hunters. Only the most daring riders had ever partnered with them, and it often ended in tragedy.

The third species were the golden dragons, Sages, a rarity since the rise of dragon hunting. Sages were the polar opposites of the Outliers: they valued peace and harmony, and they never attacked humans or other dragons. Dree wasn't even sure if they could breathe fire. They instead had the power to provide those who looked at them with feelings of contentment and joy, and still they were hunted. Dree was enraged whenever she heard of a Sage being killed. There were few left, and it was said they had fled far from any human settlements.

Finally, there were the red dragons, Flames. Flames were the ancient enemies of humans and other dragons alike, and they were dark crimson, like blood, and much larger than the other dragons. Flames considered themselves above humans and the "lesser" dragons, and history was stained with the blood of those unfortunate enough to stumble into their path. It was said that they considered humans to be locusts sweeping over the lands, which explained their merciless destruction of entire towns and villages whenever they were seen. Thankfully they rarely deigned to leave their realm deep in the mountains, where the vegetation was scarce and the rock was fire-blasted and jagged. Neither humans nor other dragons dared to venture there. Flames also breathed fire of the most insidious kind—it expanded and enveloped its targets on impact, destroying them instantly. Even Dree was afraid of Flames, and she didn't like admitting that she was afraid of anything.

Dree sighed as Lourdvang lowered himself in front of her like a languid cat.

"I'm always in trouble," Dree said grimly. She tossed the toy dragonfly on the ground, and it bounced off the rock and lay still. "It's what I do best."

"You seem different this time," Lourdvang said.

Dree watched as thick black smoke curled around his nose. It had done that since he was a baby. Dree had found him abandoned in the mountains, and she had raised him in secret, watching in awe as he grew into the magnificent creature sitting next to her. They had been like brother and sister for the past five years, and she was closer to him than anyone, except perhaps her little sister, Abigale. Of course, no one else could ever know about Lourdvang—not even Abi. Both Dree and Lourdvang would be in serious trouble if anyone found out that a dragon and a human were friends. Those days were supposed to be long over. For both of them, the penalty would be exile or death.

Dree plopped herself onto one of Lourdvang's massive feet, leaning up against his leg. She could feel the warmth permeating through him, as it always did. Most humans couldn't even touch a dragon without burning themselves and had to wear fire-resistant armor and gloves—even the riders. But Dree felt only a pleasant heat emanating from Lourdvang's scales, just like the day she had first tenderly picked him up and held him, when she found this very cave as a refuge from the cold mountain winds.

"I was fired," she said, wiping the soot from her cheeks.

"Fired?"

"Yeah," she grumbled. "I kind of . . . hit the Prime Minister with something."

Lourdvang curled his neck around to look at her, his expression amused.

"And that seemed like a good idea?"

Dree scowled. "It was an accident. Remember I told you my theory about the flying steel . . . well, I kind of tried it out."

"Did it work?"

Dree nodded, smiling. "Flew around the room! Steel flying. Can you believe it?"

"You have a gift," Lourdvang said approvingly. "One that even the clan elders say has left this world. I wish I could tell them about you, but—"

"I know."

Lourdvang looked at Dree for a moment, and then a toothy grin split his lips. "Get on."

Her eyes widened. "Really? In the daytime?"

"We'll fly east, away from the city. Out over the mountains." His blue eyes twinkled mischievously. "It's been too long since we flew together, big sister."

Dree laughed and scrambled onto Lourdvang, digging her hands into the deep grooves where the large, armorlike scales on his back met the smaller, more flexible ones on his neck. They were iron-hard and felt as hot as burning coal for most people, but Dree clenched them tightly, grinning. Dree loved flying more than anything. In the clouds, it felt like there was no memory of her life below. It was all much too far away.

"Ready?" Lourdvang growled, craning his neck to look at her.

"Ready!"

Lourdvang shot into the sky like an arrow, his gigantic, membranous wings unfurling and catching the northern wind. Dree shrieked with excitement as Lourdvang lifted them higher and higher until the hidden ledge fell away below them. As soon as Lourdvang was on the far side of the mountain, completely blocking them from the city and prying eyes, he shot forward to the east, streamlining his neck and tail and soaring over the snowcapped peaks while Dree laughed behind him.

The wind beat into her face, cold and fresh, and Dree could almost feel the soot and ash leaping off her skin and joining the black smoke that trailed from Lourdvang's mouth as he too laughed and enjoyed the evening flight. They burst above the clouds, which were glowing orange in the setting sun. It was like sailing over a lake of fire.

Dree thought back to the first time she'd flown on Lourdvang, when he was only three years old and about the size of her bedroom. Lourdvang had been shaky and unsteady, and Dree had thought she was about to die at least ten times as he spiraled through the air, but he always kept flying. By the time they had finally landed, she hadn't ever wanted to get off. For Dree, the sky was home, and Lourdvang was family.

"So you created the fire and the toy flew?" Lourdvang called over the wind.

"Yep," Dree said, closing her eyes, completely content. "It was awesome."

They soared along the southern edge of the mountains, where civilization was rapidly spreading across the countryside. Dree saw newly built roads cutting through the lush plains like rivers, dotted with carts and wagons and horses. Towns were popping up where there used to be wild country, while tilled wheat fields were replacing millennia-old forests and meadows. Everywhere, humans were expanding across the wilderness, all under the watchful eye of the celebrated Prime Minister and his cabinet. Most people loved it—the ones who were so quick to forget how things used to be. The ones who suddenly hated dragons like Lourdvang.

"They build quickly," Lourdvang said, sadness in his voice now.

"And they forget faster," Dree said, as Lourdvang wheeled back toward the mountains.

Night was falling slowly on the western horizon, creeping out of the earth. It obscured the sky enough that they could fly above the mountains, but it would be dangerous to go any closer to the towns. No one below would be able to see Dree riding the dragon, and no one would believe it even if they did. But they would see Lourdvang, and they might very well start a hunt for him. His body was a treasure of dragon parts: fangs and scales and organs.

So they stayed far from any human settlements, instead flying over the squat, snowcapped mountains and lush valleys in the range, laughing and talking like they always had. Lourdvang seemed reluctant to end the flight, and Dree certainly didn't want to head back, so they stayed up there for what seemed like hours, Dree taking in the night air and Lourdvang's sail-like wings gliding on the gentle breeze. If Dree didn't have responsibilities back home, she'd never leave the mountains.

It happened before either of them realized. Dree was busy telling Lourdvang a story about her older brother, Roshin, falling off the dock while he was staring at one of the neighbor girls. Lourdvang was chuckling at the image, black smoke spewing out of his mouth with every snort.

Dree was in the middle of describing Roshin's face as he climbed out of the water when she looked down and noticed the mountains had changed. They were jagged and sharp, their sides carved by wind and ice and devoid of any green at all. These were the Teeth, the mountains that served as the entrance to the one place in Dracone where Dree and Lourdvang did not want to be: the realm of the Flames.

"Lourdvang—"

"I see it," he said sharply, the mirth gone. He wheeled around, beating his wings urgently toward the west.

They were high up, almost in the clouds, and Dree looked around nervously, hoping they had gone unseen.

How could they have been so stupid? They'd never even dared to go near the Teeth before, and now they'd flown right over them.

"Hurry!" she urged Lourdvang.

Dree was just thinking they'd escaped unscathed when she felt an uncomfortable tingle running down her spine. It felt like someone was watching her.

She slowly turned around, knowing what she would find.

Behind them, rising up and closing in fast, were two crimson dragons, each almost double the size of Lourdvang and brimming with muscle. Fire was already flickering ominously from their mouths, red and hot and deadly. Dree knew Lourdvang could never outrun them. No one could outrun the Flames.

They pulled beside Lourdvang and growled something in their dragon language: all grunts and raspy hisses.

When they finally fell silent, Dree leaned in toward Lourdvang's ear.

"What did they say?"

When he spoke, he sounded afraid.

"They're taking us to Arncrag to meet their chieftain."

"I guess it could be worse," Dree said.

Lourdvang paused. "They're taking us there to question us before we die."

Chapter 4

Marcus hurried into his small apartment, shutting the door behind him. It was a modest place, to say the least. His uncle Jack pretty much lived at work, and he didn't come home until after nine almost every night, so he never cared to upgrade to something bigger. Jack had divorced his wife, Sheila, when he was thirty, and now she lived down in Miami with her new family that Jack didn't like to talk about. As far as Marcus knew, Jack never even considered remarrying after Sheila, and he hadn't brought a date home in the eight years that Marcus had lived with him.

"I fly stag," he always said whenever Marcus teased him about finding a wife.

Jack wasn't exactly a typical parental figure—he basically

let Marcus do whatever he wanted, whenever he wanted. It was like living with a friend . . . who just happened to be a fifty-two-year-old member of the CIA. Jack and Marcus also had one major thing in common: Neither of them believed that Marcus's father was a traitor. The accusation had isolated Jack at work. The two of them had worked together in the CIA's research department for two years before George disappeared, and they had become best friends. Jack used to say that George was like a little brother: stubborn and headstrong, but brilliant. He also said they had been working on a project together, but when Marcus asked what it was, he always said it didn't matter, as it was now defunct. Jack's favorite line was "Classified." Sometimes he said that even when Marcus asked how his day went, and then he would smirk as Marcus flushed. Marcus didn't like secrets.

When George disappeared, most people believed the stories, and they also believed that if George was a traitor, then maybe his best friend had known something too. Jack had been investigated for weeks.

Marcus felt the heat rising again, threatening to erupt. *Idiots, all of them.*

His eyes fell on a framed photograph in the hall: his burly father smiling as he held a two-year-old Marcus on his lap. There was no mother in the picture of course—Marcus's mom had died when he was a baby, and Jack didn't say much about her, except that she was already dead when he and George had met at the agency eleven years earlier. Despite that, George looked happy and kind in the picture, just like Marcus remembered him. He wasn't a traitor. He couldn't have been.

Marcus put his skateboard in the front closet and started for his room.

The apartment was sparsely decorated with a few paintings, but Jack had never put too much effort into the place. It was neat, but hardly homey. There were no photos of Jack, since most had been with Sheila and he didn't want those anymore. The kitchen was spotless and sterile, since they ate takeout almost every night. Dust sat like a blanket on one of the chairs they never used. Brian always said it looked more like a hotel than a home. Whenever Marcus went to Brian's house, he noticed how different it felt. There were family photos everywhere, the smell of dinner on the stove, siblings fighting, parents laughing. He always thought it was what a house was supposed to be like.

Unlike the rest of the apartment, Marcus's room was a mess. He plopped down in front of his laptop, which was perched on the edge of a small desk completely littered with newspaper clippings, scribbled notes, and printouts.

Everything was untidy. Clothes were strewn on the floor, half-eaten sandwiches sat on the dresser, and empty soda cans rested on the nightstand. A massive board was stuck to the far wall, covered with so many tacked-up clippings that you couldn't even tell there was a board under them anymore. They were all the same sort of odd news stories: UFO sightings in Kansas, an ever-increasing number of violent storms across the country, and Americans turning up in odd parts of the world with no recollection of how they got there.

But more than anything else, they were stories about the mysterious disappearance of George Brimley during a calamitous hurricane eight years earlier. A highly regarded CIA analyst and one of its most brilliant researchers, just gone.

Marcus felt a familiar pit form in his stomach as he stared at his father's grainy picture on one of the clippings. George had Marcus's jet-black hair, though his was streaked with gray at the temples. His eyes were an icy blue, and yet they were as warm as the deep belly laugh that Marcus remembered from when he was a little kid. The articles about George Brimley all had the same theory: He stole government secrets and ran away to Russia, where he was still living in exile. That was the widely accepted story, anyway.

Marcus knew the stories weren't true, but that didn't stop all the men in black suits from combing over every inch of their house and interviewing him at length when he was just four years old.

"Did your father ever speak any strange languages on the phone?"

"Did your father ever have any visitors?"

"Did he say where he was going that night?"

Marcus would just sit there, his hands in his lap. He had only one question.

"Where is my dad?"

Marcus knew the CIA was hiding something. He always had.

He opened the bottom drawer of his desk and withdrew his prized creation: Lightning Bug, or Bug for short. It was a drone, small and circular like the ones people attached to Go-Pros and sent flying over outdoor concerts. But Marcus had built this one from scratch with supplies and advice from Jack, who knew a lot about robotics. It had taken Marcus years to perfect it, but when it was finished, even Jack was impressed.

"Just like your father," he had said proudly. Then he turned somber, but when Marcus asked what was wrong, he just said he missed his friend. Marcus suspected that wasn't the entire story.

Still, Marcus was proud of his creation. Bug was extremely sophisticated with a complex sensor array and artificial intelligence. It was also designed for a very specific reason. Bug was built to scan and record weather patterns—specifically thunderstorms.

"Ready to get to work?" he asked tenderly, carrying Bug to the window.

Marcus spent more time with Bug than pretty much anyone other than Brian. It had a small video camera and electrostatic sensors mounted on the front, and its circular hull was a bit of a hack job of screws and uneven, bumpy welding attaching all the scrap metal he'd used from the local dump. Bug wasn't pretty, but it had been doing its job for over three years now.

And if Marcus was right about the dates, then this was its last run.

He opened his bedroom window, the wind and rain

streaming in, and put Bug on the ledge. Hurrying back to his laptop, he opened his remote program, powered Bug on, and sent it flying up into the clouds. Shutting his window, Marcus got to work.

The image was a bit grainy and obstructed by the torrential rain, so Marcus switched the view to a thermal one and saw red flashes streak across the sky. He wanted to find the center of the electrostatic activity—the heart of the storm.

As he sent Bug flying toward the city, where the lightning was flashing over Arlington's downtown core, Marcus opened his notes on his laptop. The notes had a log of every storm that had passed through Arlington County in the past eight years and the dates they fell on. He tracked the numbers and smiled.

Eight years ago the county's largest storm hit on June eighth. Seven years ago it was January seventh. And so it went on. Every year a massive storm fell on the corresponding day of the month. Last year, when it had fallen on August second, Marcus knew without a doubt that it was a countdown . . . a clock. If there was a storm the next year on the first of a month, he had to act. And today was October first.

There was no way the storm dates were a coincidence. Something was happening, and Marcus was eager to find out what they were counting down to.

As Bug continued on its course, recording electrical activity in the atmosphere, Marcus stood up and started pacing around his moss-green bedroom, his eyes locked on the storm raging outside the window. The squat oak trees lining the parking lot were billowing and twisting like tongues of fire, while leaves and trash swept across the faded concrete. What did the storms mean? What was that thing watching him in the clouds?

And did any of this have to do with his father?

Marcus dropped back into a chair and started typing in his log, feeling the anxiety and curiosity and anger welling up again. The warmth spread quickly through his fingers. Marcus looked down and scowled. He'd done it again. The computer keys were melting, the letters already heavily distorted from previous incidents. He quickly pulled his hands away. Jack hadn't been overly thrilled about buying a new Xbox—a laptop might be too much to ask. Marcus sat there for a moment, staring at his pale, slender hands.

On top of everything else, he was constantly melting things. Marcus had scoured the Web for any possible explanations, but he'd come up empty. He'd wanted to tell Jack, but something held him back. Jack had done so much for Marcus after his dad disappeared, and Marcus didn't want to freak him out. And what if Jack decided that he'd finally had enough and sent Marcus off to an orphanage or something? That was not an option.

Marcus was worried, though—worried that somehow all of it was connected. The storms, the disappearance, the fire that poured out of him. Even the mysterious aircraft.

He looked at his window again, wondering if the answer was in the storm.

His eyes widened.

Marcus slowly stood up and walked over to the window. He rested his trembling hands against the glass, staring out in disbelief.

There, hovering in a triangle and mostly obscured by the fast-moving clouds, were three triangular black objects, stark against the turbulent gray sky like drops of ink. They were completely immobile despite the wind—pointed like an arrow at the window. Marcus knew what they were now: drones. Someone was watching him.

The three drones hovered there, red eyes blazing and fixated on Marcus's apartment. On him. Marcus slowly backed away, his mind reeling. A cloud rolled by, and the drones were gone again. But he knew they wouldn't go far. He turned to his laptop.

It was time.

Dree cautiously followed Lourdvang through a massive, arched opening in the stone, high up on Arncrag, the tallest mountain of the Teeth. Arncrag was high enough that clouds hung around it, cold and damp and only adding to the terror gnawing its way through Dree's belly. She knew what was waiting for them.

They'd had no choice but to follow the two Flames back to Arncrag, despite the grim warning that they were going to be questioned there before being killed. There was a very slim chance they could talk their way out of death here, but they had no chance against two Flames in the open sky. They would have both been burned to a crisp if they tried to run. You didn't fight the Flames, you just avoided them at all costs. It was the one rule every human and dragon could agree on.

For a split second, Dree and Lourdvang had forgotten that, and now they were in serious trouble.

Dree looked around as they walked into an enormous cavern, lit only by the vestiges of gloomy sunlight that crept in through the doorway. The room smelled like fire and charred meat—she hoped it was cows or goats, and not humans. She thought back to a story her father had told her once when she was a little girl and asked about the Flames.

He was a stronger man then, but even so, he had looked afraid.

"They are reclusive," he said, turning toward the window that looked out on their old garden, back when they lived in a grand manor in the north of Dracone. "They don't often leave the Teeth and fly into the towns, since they don't have much of a taste for humans. Less meaty than moose and deer and whatever else they find in the Teeth."

Abelard turned back to her, his blue eyes hard.

"But when they do venture out to the towns and cities, death always follows. A few years ago they attacked a village to the south, Toloth, about a mile from the city. No one knows why, but they came with a terrible rage. Helvath, the chieftain, led them himself, and none survived. They say the Flames killed five hundred people that day, and it only took a few minutes."

Dree had felt her tiny hands shaking.

"What if they come here?"

Her father had taken her hand and smiled. "They won't."

"But if they do?"

He squeezed her hand reassuringly. "Then I would protect you, sweetheart. I'll always protect you."

Dree had believed him then, but that was a father who didn't even exist anymore, and regardless, he wasn't with her now. She needed to focus.

Lourdvang was stoic and silent; he had strongly advised her to stay behind him and keep her mouth shut. Flames may not have liked other dragons, but they downright hated humans. Dree knew Lourdvang would die to protect her if it came down to it, but she also knew there was nothing even a powerful dragon like Lourdvang could do if they were sentenced to death. They were at the mercy of the cruelest beings in Dracone.

Dree looked ahead and saw three dragons perched on a stone dais, their bloodred scales catching the light. The one in the center was even larger than the others. His entire body was muscle, and his black eyes flashed as they swept over Dree, small tendrils of flames flickering from his nose.

Dree knew this dragon's name from her father's stories—he was Helvath, the chieftain. He was as old as stone and apparently as bloodthirsty as they came. All dragons and humans feared him.

Few had ever met him and lived to tell the tale.

As Dree approached, she realized that the platform the dragons stood upon was not made of stone. It was bone and skull, piled in a heap beneath their terrible weight. She saw antlers and ribs and hollow sockets. Some of the skulls were human. She felt her knees buckle.

The dragon to Helvath's right, a female, was smaller, with a narrow jaw and a strange, mottled scar on her shoulder, like a bite wound. Her expression was calm and thoughtful, her eyes probing. Dree wondered who she was. On Helvath's other side was the smallest Flame, also a female with scales that were a little lighter, almost a fleshy pink, and a body less muscular and broad. Dree noticed uneasily that the third dragon's eyes seemed even more malicious than Helvath's.

They tracked her like she was a deer.

Lourdvang came to a halt in front of the platform of bones, and Dree followed suit, keenly aware that the two dragons that had escorted them here were now standing guard at the doorway, blocking any escape. She and Lourdvang were trapped.

Openings to other caverns dotted the back wall, and Dree suspected that the entire mountaintop was filled with the deadly killers. She tried to hide her shaking hands.

"Who are you?" Helvath boomed, his rasping voice shaking the cavern.

Lourdvang spoke first. "Lourdvang of the Nightwing Clan," he replied, "adopted son of Erdath II. I apologize for my accidental trespassing into your—"

"And who is the human you are with?"

Dree kept her eyes locked on the floor. "Driele Rieter."

She snuck a glance and saw Helvath staring at her, his eyes like slits.

"Rieter," he said thoughtfully, flames dancing on his lips. "Why are you here?"

"We found them in our realm," one of the dragons called from the opening. "She was riding on his back."

At this, all three dragons looked at Dree in surprise, particularly the dragon to Helvath's right—the one who had seemed a little less threatening. Now she just looked curious.

"No human has ridden a dragon in years," Helvath growled. "In fact, I believe your people have spent most of that time hunting us down. Explain."

Lourdvang went to speak, but Dree beat him to it.

"I raised him," she said quietly. "He's my brother."

Lourdvang swung his head around and glared at Dree.

"Brother?" the smallest dragon scoffed, looking at Helvath. "Kill them."

"Not yet, Cala," Helvath said, straightening up his considerable bulk and stretching. Dree watched the bulging muscles in his legs flex; curving, foot-long black claws extended from his three toes. "Do your people know about this?" he asked Lourdvang.

"No," Lourdvang replied. "I would be exiled or killed."

"Rightly so," Helvath growled. "Humans are nothing more than locusts."

"Not this one," Lourdvang said, meeting Helvath's gaze defiantly.

Dree glanced at him, grateful for the sentiment but concerned by his tone. She doubted it was a good idea to talk back to Helvath. It seemed the chieftain agreed.

"My curiosity is waning," he said coolly. "Any last—"

"Wait," the other dragon— the calm one to the right— said. She met Dree's eyes. "Are you not a bit curious about this? A human and dragon bond? And the name—"

"I did not ask you to speak, Vero," Helvath growled.

Vero nodded her head. "True. But I think we should value rare things."

Dree could tell immediately that Helvath did not agree. He snorted, fire leaping out of his nostrils, and turned back to them. "I do not value anything but my own kin."

Dree's mind was racing: She knew now they weren't getting out of the cavern alive. Images of Abi flashed before her—would her sister ever know what had happened? Would her parents look for her? There would be no trace of her when the Flames were done. She would be lost to the mountains— more forgotten bones in the valley.

Dree couldn't let that happen. She had to get back to her family.

Her hands slowly and deftly moved to her right pocket, where a little metal capsule was tucked securely against her leg. It was circular, like a ball, and filled with a black powder that Dree had been working on secretly in the shop, usually when Master Wilhelm was out. She'd had the idea while watching charcoal burn in the great furnaces in the forge, and she had tinkered with supplies from the alchemist's whenever she could. Master Wilhelm did buy supplies occasionally and often sent her to fetch them. She slowly built a store: sulfur and saltpeter, both highly flammable.

Over time, she'd begun to learn that the powder could literally create fire—but it was also extremely unstable.

When ignited, it caught fire instantly, shooting out flames in small doses and erupting in larger ones. She had never lit much at a time before, too afraid of being caught, but she had made the little canister a few months ago just in case she ever needed a distraction. Like now. She just hoped it would work—otherwise they were dead.

Dree's fingers closed around the cool metal, her eyes still locked on Helvath, who was rising to his full height now. He was as tall as the great oak trees that grew outside of the city.

Lourdvang quickly moved in front of Dree, but for all his great size, he looked miniscule next to the massive Helvath. Dree saw his hind legs shaking and knew he was afraid. Lourdvang was proud and fierce, but he was still young. He didn't want to die.

"There is only one penalty for incursion into my land," Helvath boomed, stepping down off the dais. "Death." He smiled, revealing rows of sharp teeth. "I was getting hungry."

Lourdvang prepared to fight, but Dree gently touched his leg.

"We need cover," she whispered, and felt him tense. He understood.

Helvath opened his mouth, roiling crimson fire forming in his gullet.

"Now!" Dree shouted.

She pulled the canister from her pocket just as Lourdvang blew a thick cloud of smoke through the cavern, moving like a storm on the wind. Helvath shouted something, and Dree gripped the canister, letting the latent fire flow through her hand onto a very short fuse. It caught, and she tossed it right at the three red dragons.

Chapter 6

Marcus scanned over every image of drones that he could find on the Internet, but none of them looked like the ominous machines currently hovering over his apartment building. According to what he found, drones were either small, black, and circular like Lightning Bug, or massive and white like futuristic spaceships.

If anything, the drones watching Marcus were a combination of the two: the maneuverability of the circular drones with the size and threat of the latter. They almost looked like mini stealth bombers with their angular wings and pitch-black hulls. Either way, they had to belong to the U.S. government. No one else had the technology, the resources, and the permission to sit in U.S. airspace. The CIA was watching him again, and that more than anything else told Marcus that he was close to something.

They were worried.

Marcus thought of something else: The red eyes were likely infrared, which meant even though he couldn't see the drones, they could very well be watching him right through the ceiling. They could be sourcing his Web searches. They could have hacked his entire computer already. He pushed away from the desk, his mind racing. He had to move fast.

Bug was still out there, but he had the little drone connected by a tracker to his iPhone as well. He could control it on the move and still see the data on his phone.

Marcus scooped his backpack off the floor and started stuffing some critical items into it: a flashlight, his laptop, a notepad, and, as a parting thought, an old photo of himself and his dad. He wasn't even really thinking—there wasn't time. What he was doing didn't make any sense—none of this did. And that was the point.

He glanced out his window, where the drones had vanished again. They seemed to be using the clouds as cover, but Marcus had seen their red eyes tracking his window, scanning over him. He knew they were there. And now he wanted to know why.

His dad probably wouldn't have approved of him charging out into a severe lightning storm, of course, but Marcus had waited the last seven storms out. He'd sat at his desk and wondered about the pattern and taken notes and never gotten any answers. And with every day that passed, his father's memory slipped away a little more.

No more. These weren't regular storms—they were hiding something.

Marcus had just reached for his phone when it started vibrating. Picking it up, he saw Brian's grinning picture, calling him from FaceTime. Marcus sighed and answered it, knowing that Brian would call a hundred times until he did.

"What's up?" Marcus said, distractedly checking through his backpack.

Brian looked suspicious. "Did you smash anything?"

"No," Marcus replied.

"Good. Quite the storm, huh? My mom wasn't thrilled about me coming over to play vids. And you know my dad. He said I should have been at football practice, and that he didn't believe it was canceled. The guy is crazy."

"Yeah, well, we can play vids another time," Marcus said, zipping up his bag.

"Are you doing something weird?" Brian asked. "It's just a storm."

"It's the same storm," Marcus snapped.

Brian sighed. Marcus had already told Brian about his suspicions regarding his father's disappearance and the storm that caused it. That it was exactly like the ones they'd had once a year for the past eight years.

Not a storm. A disruption.

"I know you want your dad back—"

"Yes, I do," Marcus interrupted. "And I want answers."

"And you think you're going to find them by storm chasing?"

Marcus paused. "I don't know. I didn't say it was a good idea."

"It's not an idea, period. You know what, I'm coming over. I'll sneak out."

"No," Marcus said, shaking his head. "I'm fine . . . really."

"You're sure?"

"Definitely. If it clears up in a few hours we can play vids."

Brian paused. "Fine. Brian out."

The call ended, and Marcus laughed and shook his head.

Shoving the iPhone into his jeans pocket, Marcus slung his backpack over his shoulders, tightened the straps extra securely, and went to grab his bike from the front closet. On the way, he looked over the endless news clippings on his wall.

MISSING AMERICAN WOMAN TURNS UP IN AZERBAIJAN; NO RECOLLECTION OF GETTING THERE

MYSTERIOUS OBJECT SIGHTED OVER MOOSE JAW

BLACK SPOTS IN THE SKY NEAR RIO

CIA ANALYST DISAPPEARS; QUESTIONS OF ESPIONAGE ARE RAISED

Marcus stuffed a granola bar into his pack on a whim, along with a bottle of water, and then started for the door. He was almost there when it swung open. Marcus stifled a curse.

Jack strode in through the door, drenched. His thinning blond-gray hair was plastered against his forehead while the rain dripped down his gaunt cheekbones and weak chin. He was a thin, fragile-looking man, but he was extremely intelligent.

"Decided to pop home for a bit," Jack said, taking off his jacket. "Figured I'd see if you'd been swept off somewhere." He paused. "Where are you going?"

Marcus shifted uncomfortably. "Brian's house."

"In this weather?"

"Yeah, well, it's not far."

Jack frowned as he walked into the living room, putting his briefcase on the floor.

"I see," Jack said, eyeing Marcus's backpack. "Do you want a lift?"

"No, that's all right," Marcus said quickly. "You just got home."

"There's lightning."

"I'll keep my head down."

Jack smiled. "You wouldn't happen to be analyzing storm data again, would you?"

"Of course not."

"Good. They are storms, and nothing more, Marcus."

"I know," Marcus said, staring at the floor.

"Just like your father," Jack said, sighing. "Never listening. Is Lightning Bug out there right now?"

"Maybe."

"Uh-huh. And what are the rules?"

"No trees, stay away from puddles and power lines, and I really shouldn't be on a bike. Actually the main rule is to not go outside period, so I kind of messed that up."

"Indeed." Jack started for the kitchen. "Try not to get electrocuted."

Marcus grinned. "Will do."

With that, he grabbed his bike and hurried out of the apartment. He went downstairs to the lobby, scanning the fast-moving clouds through the windows. He was looking for the center of the storm: the darkest spot in the sky. It didn't take him long to find it.

Looming over the other side of Arlington was a particularly tumultuous black cloud, roiling and twisting. He checked his phone, and sure enough Bug was hovering right below the dark spot, picking up some incredible electrical readings. The energy was off the charts. The rain was falling so heavily beneath the cloud that it looked like reality was distorted, the air curving and wavering under the downpour, and even as Marcus watched, a massive fork of lightning split through the entire cloud and lit up the sky. That was where he wanted to go.

Marcus checked his bag one more time, zipped up his hoodie, and then flung the door open, bursting into the rain and heading right for the heart of the storm.

Chapter 7

The explosion was incredible. It flashed out red and blue and yellow, erupting through the heavy smoke and lighting the room just long enough for Dree to see the three Flames leaping backward in panic. The cavern descended into darkness, and Dree quickly scrambled onto Lourdvang's back. Behind them, angry shouts filled the cave as the two dragon guards rushed into the chaos, trying to find the perpetrators.

But the cavern was huge, and in it, even Lourdvang was small. He crawled low through the smoke, and when they reached the opening, he dove straight downward, pulling his wings against his muscular flanks and dropping like a stone toward the valley floor. Dree tried not to scream while frantically wrapping her hands around his scales, her eyes still stinging from the putrid smoke. The cliff rushed by in a blur of scorched rock.

Lourdvang spotted an overhanging ledge on the side of the mountain and flew directly beneath it, huddling against the sheer rock face and using the ledge as cover. He pressed them right against the mountainside, wrapping a wing over Dree for protection.

"What are you doing?" Dree hissed, looking around in terror.

"They will expect us to run far and fast. They will not look for us here."

"So how do we escape?" she asked, frowning.

The sun was just visible to the west, sending its last golden rays into the Teeth. Lourdvang looked out over the barren mountains.

"We wait for darkness."

Dree and Lourdvang waited until the night had crept over the mountains like a fog, obscuring the peaks and lighting the sky with millions of stars. They sat mostly in silence as they listened to the Flames raging overhead, scouring the skies and sending fire screaming in all directions. Dree suspected no one had ever escaped their lair before, never mind attacked their chieftain.

She shuddered to think what would happen to her and Lourdvang if they were caught.

Whispering to each other, Dree and Lourdvang discussed their options, but Dree sensed that something was a bit off. Lourdvang replied in only one or two words, and his eyes were always outward, away from her. She wondered what was wrong.

The waiting gave Dree a lot of time to think, but as usual that was no comfort. If she wasn't busy, the memories returned. Sometimes she thought of Gavri, playing in the yard, his hair like straw in the sun as he chased a tiny Abigale around. He was two years younger than Dree, kindhearted and quiet. Her mother had always favored him, maybe because he loved to help her in the garden. He said it was because he loved the feeling of the soil.

Dree could still hear him screaming from down the hall. Every time, she remembered the same moment: She couldn't get to him, and her father was grabbing her and the ceiling was falling and there was so much smoke. But the fire didn't hurt her. She could have gotten to him. She could have saved him. She had to.

After all, it was Dree who started the fire.

When the cover of darkness finally fell, Lourdvang slipped out from under the overhanging ledge and glided through the valleys, staying at the base of the Teeth, where the deepest shadows could hide them. The night air was bitingly cold, and Dree dug her fingers into Lourdvang's scales for warmth, icy tears streaming from her eyes and across numbed cheeks.

They glided for what seemed like hours in and out of the

jagged mountains, listening for the sounds of pursuers from above. It was terrifying—waiting for a dark eclipse against the night sky. But it was silent in the Teeth, other than the echoing calls of the few animals brave enough to live there. It was a long and eerie flight, and when they finally emerged from the Flames' realm, back to where the mountains were fuller and squatter and covered with some greenery, they both relaxed. As Lourdvang gained altitude and headed back to the secret cave near the city, Dree finally had to ask.

"Is something wrong?"

Lourdvang paused for a long time. "What was that weapon?"

Dree immediately understood.

"Something I created," she said softly.

"In the shop?"

"Yes," she replied, feeling a little defensive. "Just something I did on my own."

"A weapon to kill dragons."

Dree scowled. "A weapon, period. You know I don't want to kill any dragons. Though I wouldn't have complained if that one took out Helvath."

"It's powerful," Lourdvang said. "Do any other humans have it?"

"Of course not! I didn't share anything useful with Wilhelm. Swords, spears, and axes were all I made for him."

Again, Lourdvang was silent for a moment. "If humans had the weapon you used today, they could probably wipe out the dragons once and for all. They would have mastered fire."

"They won't get it from me," Dree said coolly, insulted that Lourdvang could ever think she would put the dragons in danger.

Lourdvang didn't reply, and they flew back to his cave in silence. Dree climbed off his back, nodded farewell, and stormed off toward the city, tired and cold and angry. She made the long walk down the mountain as quickly as she dared, stepping over divots and holes and then setting off across the meadow. The tall grass reached almost to her waist, and in the darkness her legs seemed to disappear into it. Dree jogged through the city outskirts toward the docks, and she heard the slurred shouts from drunks in the taverns. The wealthy Draconians, the ones with the fanged earrings and half-shaven heads and elaborate flame-resistant armor, strolled along the city streets, laughing and letting their leather boots clomp off the stones. They didn't seem to have a care in the world.

And why should they? They lived in stone manors and drank wine from the south and never worried about whether they could afford to put food on the table.

They didn't have to live on the docks.

Dree soon arrived at her home, nestled in the sprawling, dirty splotch of wooden shacks perched on the edge of the lake. There were too many people for too small of a place: The little huts were basically built against one another, their ragged curtains pulled tight to afford what little privacy was possible. The roads were tired stone, cracked and worn, and everything smelled like fish. It was a tough place, but it was home.

Dree eased her front door open, sneaking in like a stray

shadow. The smells of charred wood from the fireplace and goat stew wafted over her nose. Her mother had probably left some in the pot for her, hardening now to congealed paste. She made it right through the small main room and into her bedroom, relieved she hadn't woken her parents. They had probably just assumed Master Wilhelm kept her working late, which wouldn't have been a first. She didn't have the energy to tell them what had happened, and besides, they were sleeping. She needed sleep too, if she could get it. It had been a rough night.

Dree turned to her cot and saw that Abigale was snuggled under the thick covers, obviously waiting for her. Abi slept in another equally small bedroom beside Dree's, nestled on bunks with their little brothers Marny and Otto. Dree used to share her bedroom with her old brother, Rochin, but he had left the family a year prior and now lived in a small apartment downtown, totally immersed in the new Dracone.

That meant Dree had a whole bedroom to herself, tiny as it was, though Abi spent almost every other night in there anyway, huddling beside Dree for protection against the cool, damp air that hung by the lake at night and crept beneath their blankets.

Seeing Abi in the faint moonlight reminded her of a night many years earlier.

Abi had been asleep in the little shelter her family had found themselves in after the fire, tucked into the corner away from all the strangers. Dree crept over to her sister and gently laid her hands on Abi's arm. She knelt there, the moonlight playing tricks around her like glimpses of the dead, and made a solemn promise.

"I will never, ever let anything happen to you," Dree whispered, tears running freely down her cheeks. "I promise you that I will protect you, Abi. I will keep you safe."

Dree swore to herself that she wouldn't let what happened to Gavri ever happen to Abi. Dree had loved her brother, and she had let him die. No . . . she had killed him. Dree couldn't bring Gavri back, but she could protect Abi with everything she had—to death if need be. Since that day in the shelter, Dree had kept her promise, and she would continue to. Sometimes it was the only thing that kept her here, instead of off permanently in the mountains with Lourdvang.

Dree sighed and climbed into bed next to her little sister, watching the faint moonlight creep through the curtains once again, dancing along the rotting wooden slats on the ceiling. She ran her hand through her sister's matted hair. She had lost her job, and now her family would be struggling more than ever to put food on the table. Dree felt sick when she thought of Abi having to get a job at ten like she had, when she should have been at school. *I won't let that happen*, Dree promised herself, nestling close to her little sister and closing her eyes. She would figure something out.

⊕

Daylight dawned all too soon, spilling into Dree's bedroom and lighting up the swirling clouds of dust and dirt. Dree blinked awake, feeling like she had only just closed her eyes. For a second, she forgot all about the traumatic events of the previous night, but she was almost instantly assaulted by images of a toy dragonfly, a Prime Minister, and terrifying red dragons. A part of her had hoped it was all just a dream.

She thought of Lourdvang and instantly felt guilty for being angry with him. Of course he would ask about the weapon; it was his kind that was in danger. Dree decided that she would go up to the cave and apologize later. First, though, she had to speak to her parents. Her stomach clenched, and she stared up at the ceiling, feeling nauseated. She was not looking forward to their reactions, their disappointment.

"You're back," a quiet voice said, and she turned to see her sister staring at her.

Abi had Dree's blue eyes, though Abi's were soft and comforting. Her chestnut hair was long and usually tangled, since neither Dree nor her mother had the time to comb it, and Abi didn't care enough to do it herself. And where Dree's features were hard—strong brow, high cheekbones, a bump on her nose from when she'd broken it in a fistfight—Abi's face was delicate and instantly warmed by a smile.

"I am," Dree replied. "You were waiting?"

Abi grinned. "I was." Her smile faltered. "I kind of . . . looked around while I was in here. I was bored, and I shouldn't have, but I looked under the bed."

Dree stiffened. "You did what?"

Abi pulled a small black-iron figurine from beneath the covers, welded with incredible detail from extra scraps at the forge. It portrayed a Nightwing with a rider on its back, held in place by a saddle and armor plating. It was a perfect to-scale replica of something Dree had been designing for months, and it wasn't the only creation hidden under her bed. There were miniature replicas of weapons—projectiles and bows and jousts—all designed for use from the back of a dragon. But Dree knew why Abi had selected this one in particular: Any mention of dragon riding was forbidden. To create new technology for dragon riding would have landed Dree in prison . . . or worse.

Of course, Abi didn't know the half of it—these inventions weren't just for any rider and dragon, they were for Dree and Lourdvang. They were acts of war.

Abi looked at Dree, eyebrows raised. "Why didn't you tell me you were doing all this?"

Dree snorted. "Why do you think?"

"You can trust me, you know," Abi said, crossing her arms.

Dree smiled and wrapped an arm around her sister.

"Of course I can," she said. "But the less people who know, the better. You know what would happen if the Protectorate saw this. The generals. I would be thrown in prison or . . ." She trailed off.

"Then why do it?" Abi whispered.

Dree paused. She couldn't tell her sister about Lourdvang. It was too dangerous.

"Because of Dad," Dree replied, which was partly true.

"Now, you can't tell anyone—"

"Dree!" her mother called from the kitchen. "Get up for work."

Dree sighed, staring up at the ceiling.

"What's wrong?" Abi asked.

"You'll see."

It wasn't pretty. Dree's mother was furious, storming around the living room and probably waking up every single person on the docks. The few paintings they had on the walls—relics of a time when the family lived in a beautiful house in the city, her parents the descendants of two prominent families—rattled and shook, threatening to fall. Dree's father watched in silence from his ratty old armchair, the fabric stained and worn. His brow was furrowed, but he showed no other expression. He just studied the proceedings carefully.

"How do you 'just' get fired?" her mom asked again, her voice getting louder. "You must have done something."

Dree couldn't tell her mom the real reason. Her father was the only one who knew about the fire, and he had forbidden her a long time ago from telling anyone, even her mother. He said she wouldn't understand, that she would be afraid. Dree wouldn't blame her.

"I don't know," Dree murmured, sitting at the kitchen table, which was perched in the center of the house. "He just said I was fired. He said he didn't like my attitude."

"There's a surprise," her mother snarled.

Katrine Reiter was a beautiful woman who had been worn down by a hard life. Her blond hair, frizzy and unkempt, was graying, while her once delicate features were now marred by dark circles under her eyes and wrinkles that sprouted from her lips like cracks in the cobblestone. She worked at a mill on the outskirts of the city, lugging steel and firing coal and a bunch of other things the daughter of a wealthy merchant should never have had to do. Dree and her mother weren't close. Dree suspected that her mother had never quite forgiven her—no matter how she might have tried—for the loss of Gavri.

Katrine didn't know what had happened, but she had seen Dree screaming that fateful day. She had heard her for years after in the middle of the night, tossing and mumbling and crying out for her little brother. Apologizing. She must have known it was Dree's fault. The coldness that crept into her voice sometimes was proof enough.

The memory of Gavri crept up again. Dree shook it away. *Not now.*

"I'm sorry," Dree whispered.

Her mother relented just a little at that and stopped pacing.

"Well, I suggest you go apologize to Wilhelm and see if he'll take you back." She paused. "And if not, I'm sure there are other jobs out there. I have to go to work." She spit the word *work* like an insult, and Dree wondered if that was directed at her father as well. He did shift slightly in his chair. "I hope to hear some good news when I get back."

With that, Katrine stormed out of the house, slamming the door and leaving a miserable Dree sitting alone with her father and a very sympathetic-looking Abi. Marny and Otto were fighting in the bedroom.

"I better go," Dree said, climbing to her feet.

"Wait," her father said gently. "Come here."

Dree walked over, staring at her father with a mixture of love and anger. She wasn't angry that he was injured, she was angry that he didn't seem to want to get better. That he just spent his days miserable in his armchair, watching the boats come into the docks. She was angry that he wasn't the man she remembered as a child. The strong man with deep blue eyes. The warrior. The dragon rider.

He had been among the greats, protecting the skies on the back of his dragon, Delpath. He came from a long line of dragon riders, ancient and respected, and he had carried on the name proudly. But when the purge of the dragons started, the riders were outlawed and Abelard was stripped of his property and wealth—called a traitor instead of a hero. She knew from Rochin's stories that he cared less about the money than losing his dearest friend, Delpath.

But even after the purge, he had remained strong. He had become a leader in Dracone, a voice of discontent and even revolution. Abelard had spoken out against the dragon hunters and the growing economic disparity. But when his back gave out while loading ships on the docks one day, so did his inner strength. Something within him broke that day, and he had never been the same since.

But Dree also loved her father desperately. He was the calm voice and the tender heart that tempered her mother. And so Dree let him take her hand, her eyes meeting his.

"You did something," he said. It wasn't a question.

"Yes."

He nodded. "Did he see it? Wilhelm?"

"No. Only Sasha, and he didn't see me do it. He just saw it flying."

"Flying?" her father asked, looking confused.

Dree shrugged. "I kind of made a flying dragonfly out of steel. And then it landed on the Prime Minister's head."

Her father laughed, a rare sound over the past few years. "I won't even ask. Was he angry?"

"Not really. Wilhelm was though. He loves the Prime Minister."

"Everyone does." Abelard pulled Dree close, lowering his voice to a whisper. "You have a gift, Dree. That fire is matched only by what's up here," he said, tapping on her forehead. She couldn't help but smile. "You'll have a chance to use it, I'm sure. But for now, keep your head down. Get your job back."

He squeezed her hand and leaned back, shrinking into the fabric again. Dree nodded, fighting unexpected tears that threatened to escape. Where did he go when his proud chin fell and his eyes drifted toward the window, fogging over like the lake in the morning?

"Thanks, Dad."

She gave Abi a quick hug and headed out the door,

jamming her hands into her pockets. It wasn't fair. The girl who could create fire from her hands and make steel fly and challenge the red dragons had to go beg Master Wilhelm for forgiveness.

Keep your head down, she thought bitterly. *I've been doing that my whole life.*

She turned onto the main street, scowling. It didn't matter.

It was time to go find a job.

Chapter

Marcus pedaled frantically down the street, barely able to open his eyes against the pounding rain. He didn't see any drones, but he had a feeling they weren't far away.

The sky was bursting with energy—clouds roiling and twisting and stretching across the sky like fingers while lightning split the darkness. The electrostatic readings from Bug, which was still up in the clouds, were beyond anything Marcus had seen in all his research. He risked another glimpse at his cell phone. This storm was different, stronger. It was just as he had guessed: The storms were a clock, and they were counting down to today. But why? What would he find in the heart of the storm? And would he even make it there alive?

Either way, Marcus was going to test his one and only theory. He had to try.

Turning onto a busy street, Marcus pedaled even harder, rain pouring down his face. He knew he looked like a drowned rat, and he could see cars driving by with people shaking their heads at anyone stupid enough to be outside in this weather. They didn't know the half of it. It was about to get stupider.

The lightning was flashing like a strobe light now, the deluge so thick that even the many disapproving faces were blurred. Marcus could barely see where he was going, but he was riding on pure instinct: *Get to the heart of the storm*. He had a feeling he would know what to do when he got there.

Scanning the sky for drones, Marcus thought back to the day his dad had left.

The memory was vague, maybe as much his imagination as anything else. The windowpanes were rattling, and Marcus remembered the branches of the oak behind their house scratching against the glass like fingers. He was in the living room, watching his favorite movie, *The Wizard of Oz*. Marcus had seen the movie dozens of times—he and his father had watched it for as long as Marcus could remember. George loved the movie, and he passed that love down to Marcus. He used to sit with Marcus on his lap, and at least once during the film, he would lean in and whisper, "Remember, if you can weather the storm, you'll find home on the other side." Marcus never thought anything of it—he was more interested in the flying monkeys. It would be years before Marcus realized that maybe there was something more to his father's words. A clue.

That night, though, Marcus was watching the movie alone. Dorothy's house had just been swept up in the clouds, and she was staring out in disbelief as her former life floated by, followed soon after by the witch.

She was bringing the past with her, good and evil.

The doorbell rang, and Marcus almost jumped off the couch. He suddenly heard thumping footsteps from down the hall, and his dad appeared in the hallway, pulling on a Windbreaker and forcing a smile that even Marcus thought was weird. He pulled open the door, and Jack hurried inside, wiping his foggy glasses.

His father grabbed Jack's hand, shaking it a lot more tightly than usual.

"Thanks, Jack," George said quietly. "I'll be back soon."

Jack nodded. "I'll keep an eye on him; don't worry."

Marcus started to get up, sensing that something was wrong, but his father walked over to him and laid a strong hand on his shoulder. He smiled again.

"I have to run to the office for a bit," he said.

"Why?" Marcus asked. "It's nighttime."

"There's a problem. I'll be back soon—don't worry."

He paused for a moment and then gave Marcus a little shake, noticing his son's worried look as he stared at the raging storm outside their window.

"A little storm never stopped Dorothy, did it?"

Marcus smiled. "No."

"And it won't stop us either. See you soon, son. Try not to fly to Oz tonight."

And just like that, he was out the door, not looking back even once. The door was almost blown off its hinges when he opened it, and then Marcus watched as two red taillights faded into the night. The police found the car later on the out-skirts of the city, abandoned. They never found any trace of George Brimley, though—no sign of struggle, no DNA out-side the car. Nothing. It was like he had never even existed.

Marcus veered right and narrowly avoided a fire hy-drant. He risked a wipe to his glasses, which were completely fogged over, and looked up to see that the dark cloud was al-most over him. There was another brilliant flash of lightning.

And then he felt a familiar tingling down his spine.

Glancing back, Marcus saw something drop below the clouds. Red eyes.

At least five of the drones were overhead, tracking him across the city. Whatever Marcus was about to find, it was clear the drones were trying to stop him. Marcus wondered if he was actually in danger this time. A tingling heat raced through him, his stomach twisting like a pretzel.

He biked as hard as he could, sloshing around in his Adidas. He was soaked to the bone and freezing, but he didn't care. The massive black cloud was almost right over him.

The drones flew lower, like a flock of birds. They moved silently, eerily, staying in close formation. They were almost serene, but Marcus knew they were probably loaded with weap-onry. At any moment, they could decide to blow him to pieces.

Cursing, he weaved out onto the road and back to the sidewalk again before wheeling down a side street, trying to lose them. But it was useless. The drones were always above him, slowly descending like an arrow pointed at his back. He waited for the end. For the flash of light. Desperate, Marcus made one last dash for the center of the storm, thinking for just a moment how crazy it was that he was chasing a cloud.

Especially one that was shooting forks of lightning out toward the ground.

"Leave me alone!" he shouted as a drone slipped into his vision.

It was even larger than he thought, probably the size of a fighter jet. It was as black as night, and its crimson eye seemed almost *alive*, flicking over to him like it was studying his every move. That's when Marcus noticed the symbol.

It was painted onto the black hull, just slightly visible in the storm. One large rectangle and two smaller ones on either side. And above the smaller rectangles: eyes.

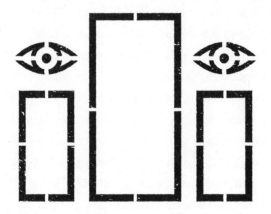

He had seen that symbol once before . . . sort of. When his father had first disappeared, Marcus snuck into his study—a place that had always been strictly off-limits.

It was mostly empty, aside from a few scribbled notes and work files. But there, carved into the wooden desk, were three rectangles. The same ones Marcus was staring at now, but without the eyes watching overhead.

Was it a warning from his father? And what were those ominous eyes?

The drone flew closer again, now barely ten feet away. It was right beside Marcus, almost forcing him off the street. Marcus turned back to the road.

Why were the drones flying so low? Were they trying to take him alive? Or were they just trying to stop him from reaching the center of the storm?

Whatever their plan was, it wouldn't work. He lifted his head and found himself right beneath the darkest part of the sky, where the lightning was almost constant.

Suddenly, a drone wheeled in front of Marcus, blocking his path. He shouted and wrenched his handle to the right, teetering off balance and heading straight for a waiting tree. But he never made impact.

There was a blinding flash of electric blue, fizzling and crackling and strangely warm, and then Marcus had the distinct sensation of flying off his bike.

He caught a glimpse of white light and immediately realized what had happened.

He'd been struck by lightning.

He was dead.

Chapter 9

Dree trudged down the street toward city center, disheartened and bitter. She had spent yesterday flying on the back of a dragon, and today she was going to go back to the forge to grovel at Master Wilhelm for her underpaid job back. Well, that or beg someone else to take her on instead. She had a feeling Wilhelm wouldn't be overly forgiving.

Even though I'm twice the welder he is, she thought.

Her stomach growled, and she realized she hadn't even thought to grab breakfast before she left. There wouldn't have been much to choose from: stale bread, moldy potatoes, or a mash of wheat and grains called lavash that her mom made, but it was better than nothing. She certainly didn't have the money to go buy anything from one of the merchants or vendors in the market. And that was before she was fired.

As she approached downtown Dracone—the raucous morning noise already echoing around her—she looked around, envious of her surroundings. Dracone became progressively nicer as one headed downtown, where the houses were large and manicured and every now and then an enormous mansion was perched on the side of the street, gleaming and palatial. Metal was the new trend now, forged into massive doors and pillars or slapped against wood and brick for no reason. It was the hot new material—it was the future.

The mills and forges were churning out new products, and the people loved it.

The mansions Dree passed housed the wealthy citizens of Dracone. These were the new capitalists who invested in roads and bonds and traded in the thriving dragon market: fangs and scales and even great black hearts, which were thought to bring power to those who ate them. It was disgusting, but it was the way things were now.

It didn't used to be like this. Dracone's elite used to be royals or generals, and especially the old dragon-rider families, like Dree's, whose riches had been passed down for generations. They were respected and generous—they cared about the poor and built schools and hospitals. There was a thriving middle class back then, and the ancient families felt responsible for the city and its people, working with the king to ensure that food and water were available for everyone. Now Dracone's most powerful citizens were the businesspeople who cared only about money. The downtown core thrived, while the poor slums were forgotten. For the downtrodden, there was nothing but rats and fetid lake water.

Dree watched as a woman walked past, wearing an onyx chest plate and twin fang earrings. Half of her hair was shaved off, and the other half was dyed crimson. If she noticed Dree, she didn't show it. The rich didn't look at the poor, unless it was with disdain or annoyance, like how they might look at an inconveniently placed puddle.

Dree scowled, her mood darkening. Why should she be the ignored one? She could ride dragons and had fire in her skin—she should have been a rider instead of a beggar.

Her eyes fell on the great mountains in the distance. If it wasn't for Abi, she would leave right now. She would live with Lourdvang in the mountains and forget about everything down in Dracone. But she had a family to take care of.

As she walked, Dree looked with disdain at some of the wooden stands that had been set up in the more suburban areas—obviously by merchants hoping to catch the wealthy citizens on their way to work. Her eyes fell on one large stand in particular, and she stopped immediately. Without thinking, she stormed over, enraged.

A bowl was perched there, catching the rays of the morning sun and sparkling magnificently. It looked to have been forged of several pieces of gold, overlapping one another, not quite creating a smooth surface. When she picked it up, the bowl was extremely heavy and as hard as iron. She knew it. It wasn't made of gold, it was made of dragon scales.

"Do you have the money for that bowl, girl?" the merchant, a grotesque older woman with heavy eyeliner and no eyebrows, asked, rising from her chair.

"Is this new?" Dree asked quietly.

"I should hope so," the merchant snarled. "They killed the dragon three days ago. Cost me a fortune for just a few scales, which is why I will be selling it for a fortune as well. Now hand it over, girl. You look like a stray dog in clothes— you can't afford that."

She snatched the bowl out of Dree's hands and carefully put it back in its place.

Dree stood there, bristling. She longed to put her hand on the haphazard wooden frame and burn the entire stand to the ground. But she would just end up in prison, and the scales wouldn't even be touched. What did it matter anyway? The Sage was already dead—killed because of human greed. It probably hadn't even fought back. Dree felt sick.

Leaving the stand, she started for Wilhelm's Forge, scowling and muttering.

"You people make me sick," she said, looking around. "All of you."

She hadn't made it far when a sudden gust of wind picked up, blowing a cloud of dust across the road. Dree frowned and covered her eyes as the wind grew even stronger, pushing her sideways. Dirt and trash roared past Dree, and she heard people shouting, though she could barely open her eyes to see them. Just as she was stumbling toward the far side of the street, looking for cover, she heard a startled gasp and caught a glimpse of a boy rolling hard across the cobblestone street. The howling wind stopped instantly, as if it had never been there, and Dree lowered her hands.

Her eyes fell on the boy, lying sprawled out on the road and soaked to the bone. He was dressed unlike anyone she had ever seen: a green short-sleeved shirt, dark blue pants that seemed a bit too tight, and orange shoes that looked like striped flowers. He had unusual gray eyes, and his mop of ebony hair matched the thick frames of his glasses, while his face was pale and peaked, with light freckles on his nose.

Marcus looked around, his eyes wide. He turned to Dree and frowned.

"Am I dead?" he whispered.

"Uh . . . no," she said.

He quickly climbed to his feet and tried to walk, but instead did a little wobble and almost pitched backward onto the street. Dree grabbed his arm and steadied him.

"Are you all right?" she asked, still examining his strange attire.

"Not . . . sure," he managed. "How can this . . . I knew it! But who are you? Where am I? How is this possible?"

Dree raised her eyebrows, examining the clearly insane boy in front of her. She was tempted to just leave him there, but he seemed helpless and lost. Sighing, she pulled him toward a back alley where he could lean against the wall and get his bearings without people constantly bumping into him. The crowd was already hurrying past again, shooting him bewildered looks when they saw his clothes and then continuing on.

Dree led Marcus to the alley and straightened him up. He started to regain his composure, and he scanned over the chaotic street. Shops and homes were tucked closely together, brick and gray stone, while the people wore a mixture of bizarre outfits and wool peasant clothes. The smells assaulted his nostrils: smoke and sweat and worse.

"Interesting," he said. "It's like the Industrial Revolution here. Is that a smokestack?"

"Who are you?" Dree asked.

Marcus turned back to her, and for the first time took a closer look at the girl standing in front of him. She was wearing coarse brown clothes and hide boots, while her exposed arms were sun-kissed and formed like tempered steel. Normally, a girl like that would have caused him to go as red as a fire hydrant and forget how to speak English, but he was a bit preoccupied at the moment. She was very pretty though—like a warrior elf character out of Dungeons & Dragons. Brian would have passed out.

"Marcus. Where am I? What's your name?"

"Dree," she replied, watching him closely as he took an object out of his pocket and checked it. "And you're in Dracone."

"An alter-world? I knew it! Do you know a George—"

He suddenly stopped, his eyes narrowing.

"What's wrong?" Dree asked.

Marcus stepped past her, still staring up at the sky. "Impossible."

Dree followed his gaze. Far ahead, just below one of the

scattered clouds that was lazily drifting across the morning sky, were two black dots. They seemed to be floating. Each had a red eye blazing like a furnace and watching the city below, unblinking. Dree instantly thought of dragons, but the objects didn't seem to be moving. Instead, the clouds just rolled over them like water over a stone. As she squinted for a better view, she saw three more shapes, as white as the clouds and almost invisible in the daylight. They were larger than the red-eyed ones, though they had the same triangular shape and seemed just as motionless. They were all just waiting above the city. Watching.

"What are those things?" Dree asked.

He never got a chance to answer. A streak of light filled the sky, and then one of the shops across the street exploded into a massive fireball.

Dree and Marcus staggered backward as a cloud of debris swept over the block, spraying the busy street with fragments of wood and brick. There was a brief moment of silence as the darkness blocked out the sun, and then screams erupted everywhere as people picked themselves up and saw the massive crater where a shop had once been. Dree looked up and saw the black and white shapes dropping toward the city, moving in a perfect triangle. They moved gracefully—no flapping wings or tails or feet. Just silent death.

Marcus heard a sudden burst of noise cut through the city like the frantic beating of a drum. The drones had switched to their machine guns, and they were leveling the neighborhood.

Marcus pushed past Dree, his eyes on the sky.

"What are they doing?" he said faintly.

As they watched, the drones continued their attack. Houses and buildings burst apart or collapsed. People were gunned down relentlessly as they tried to run away. The drones were laying utter waste to the city, and they were doing so directly on a path to Marcus and Dree.

"I would be more concerned with what they're *about* to do," Dree snapped, grabbing Marcus's arm and pulling him into the alley. "We need to go."

"Where?"

She looked around, trying to get her bearings. Her brother Rochin lived only a few blocks away, in an apartment building on the edge of the downtown core.

It would have to do.

"Follow me," she said, starting down the narrow alley. She looked back and saw Marcus still staring out at the drones. "Now!" she shouted.

He jerked and took off after her, the sounds of screaming following close behind them. Dree hadn't heard screams like that in years. Not since the day of the fire.

Marcus looked back and saw the drones make another pass over the city, moving in perfect formation. Another brick house was cut to ribbons.

Why are they attacking? he thought. *Are they searching for me?*

Dree and Marcus rounded a corner and burst across a busy street, where people were running frantically in all directions to escape the onslaught. Armor-clad soldiers came charging down from the local barracks, but as soon as they saw the source of the attack, they stopped and stared at the drones in obvious confusion, lowering their swords and spears with uncertainty. None of them moved.

"Get the dragon weapons!" the commander shouted.

That meant catapults and bows and snares. Dree doubted they would work against the flying machines. *Flying steel.* She had known it could work, but not like that.

She led them to Rochin's apartment building and threw the front door open, allowing Marcus to rush inside ahead of her. They flew up two flights of concrete steps before sliding to a halt in front of her brother's door, knocking frantically.

"Rochin!" Dree shouted. "Rochin!"

She hadn't seen him in months. She thought back to the day he'd left.

"It's not right," her mother had said, wringing her hands together. "You're only seventeen, Roch. You don't even have a job. Your sisters need you—"

Dree was watching from her room with Abi, who was in tears. She loved Rochin.

"I won't stay here for another minute," Rochin snarled. He already looked half-gone. His eyebrows were shaved into straight lines, his hair crimson.

Dree's father watched from his chair, not speaking.

"Why not?" her mother asked.

He laughed cruelly. "Why? Look around, Mom. We live in a shack. The world is building up around us, and we're sinking into the lake. This place is pathetic."

Dree heard the pain in her mother's voice. "This is our *home*. It hasn't been easy."

"It's *your* home," Rochin said, opening the door. "I'm tired of hearing about how great our lives used to be. How Dad was some important dragon rider. What are we now? The dragons are being wiped out. That time is over. I'm ready for something new."

Dree sat on the bed, her arm around Abi. It wasn't fair—her brother could just run away and leave everything behind: the cold that crept in through the floorboards, the constant fighting coming from her parents' bedroom, the father that was slipping away.

"Are you going to say anything?" Dree's mother asked, looking at Abelard.

He was silent for a moment. "No."

"Of course not," Rochin said. "I'd say I'll miss you, Dad, but I haven't seen the real you in years." He hesitated, and his hard blue eyes softened when he found Dree and Abi in their room. "Goodbye."

The door slammed as Rochin left, and the house fell into silence.

Now the door instantly flew open, Dree's disheveled brother on the other end looking like he'd just woken up, which he almost certainly had. From what Dree heard, all he did was sleep and party and scrape money together where he could, hauling steel and stone to the construction crews. He hadn't been back to the house once.

He looked at Dree with frantic eyes, and he had a bag

in his hand, half-packed.

"Where are you going?" she asked.

"The bunkers," he said. "Where do you think?"

They could still hear the thudding of machine guns and the terrified screams from the streets. Dree frowned. The bunkers were on the other side of the city—ancient stone structures built as a defense against the dragon attacks of old. But it would take at least a half hour to get there, and they'd have to venture out into the open streets to do it. She knew that was not a good idea.

"What are you doing here?" Rochin asked suddenly, looking at Marcus.

Marcus shifted a little under his distracted gaze. Rochin looked a little like Dree, but like a blurry reflection in the water: pale blue eyes that barely seemed to focus, sandy blond hair standing on end, and eyebrows singed into short, straight lines like they had been drawn on with a marker. He wore only his pants, revealing a strong, sun-weathered chest marked with blisters and burns.

"Trying to take shelter," Dree said impatiently. "You'll never make it to the bunkers. Can we—"

Before she could finish, the back of Rochin's apartment was suddenly shredded by machine gun fire shattering the windows and decimating the thick concrete walls. Screams erupted through the apartment building as it was attacked, and one of Rochin's teenaged roommates emerged from a bedroom, crawling across the floor and shrieking as the walls collapsed around him in a cloud of dust.

Rochin looked back, paused, and then pushed past Dree, sprinting down the hall.

"Get to shelter!" he called behind him.

Dree scowled. Running as always . . . and leaving her behind. Her older brother might have been a coward, but she wasn't.

Dree scrambled into the swirling debris to help Rochin's roommate, whom she remembered as Olli. In the months before he left the family, Rochin had introduced them to his new friends. Olli grabbed desperately onto Dree's hand, blinking in the dust and grabbing at a small wound on his leg. Marcus hurried over and helped pull the boy to his feet, letting him lean heavily on his shoulder. Olli was extremely unsteady as they started toward the front door, and Marcus looked back, nervous.

The gunfire had stopped, but Marcus knew that didn't mean the drones were gone. He left Olli with Dree for a moment and tentatively walked over to the jagged, blown-out hole that used to be a window, scanning over the skyline. He couldn't see any drones, neither close by nor over the crumbling southern end of the city, where smoke and screams still floated into the air. Perhaps the drones had done enough destruction for one day. Marcus was just turning back to help Olli when he looked straight up. There, just below the clouds, he saw a massive white shape floating above the building, a red-eyed drone beside it. He realized now that the white drones were far larger than the black ones and seemed to be packing even heavier firepower. Whereas the red-eyed drones seemed to be made for tracking and gunning down specific targets, the white ones were like heavy bombers, designed for mass destruction. Now, though, they were simply watching, letting the clouds drift past them.

It was exactly what they were doing when they had first appeared in Dracone . . . right before they fired.

"Run!" he shouted, starting for the door.

They had just reached the hallway when a massive explosion rocked the building.

Chapter 10

The floor shook violently as cracking and splintering noises raced through the walls. Dragging Olli to the staircase, Marcus and Dree exchanged a terrified look. Both of them understood—the building was coming down. Fast.

They raced down the concrete stairs as quickly as possible—Olli struggling to walk—and Dree led them out into a side alley. Marcus looked up and saw that the drones were gone again—vanished into the cloudscape like phantoms. But he knew they could be back at any second.

"We need to move," he said, pulling the limping Olli down the alley.

They were just in time. Another earsplitting crack burst into the air, and the three of them looked back in horror as the entire building shifted. Then, with a last horrific wrench of steel and wood and concrete, the building collapsed. A massive tidal wave of debris erupted outward, covering the surrounding area in dust that swept over them. Marcus and Dree both turned away, covering their eyes with their hands. Dree couldn't even comprehend what she was seeing. The city was in ruins.

They stood there for a moment, looking like freshly carved statues. Marcus looked up at the now-empty sky. Why had the drones attacked the city? What was their goal in killing all those people?

Despite all the questions, Marcus was sure of one thing: he was to blame for all of this. He had brought the drones to Dracone.

The soot-stained families running down the streets with bundled children in their arms, the ruined shops and homes, the screams that filled the air like horrible music—it was his fault. He watched as the dust settled onto the shattered streets and realized that he was very, very far from home.

Dree and Marcus left an overcrowded hospital, which was teeming with soot-covered, injured civilians, crying families, and white sheets. The small waiting room had smelled like charred flesh, and Marcus had barely managed not to vomit as he sat in there, waiting for someone to help Olli. Even now that he was outside in the fresh air, Marcus felt sick to his stomach.

He wasn't sure if it was the stench or the guilt.

The attack had stopped as suddenly as it had started. It seemed the apartment building was the last target of the murderous drones. For now, anyway.

Olli was receiving treatment inside, along with the scores of others. For Dree, the waiting room had been unbearable as well. Everywhere she looked she saw Gavri—his blue eyes watching her from the corners. He was crying on the hospital bed, holding his sides. He was looking at her from beneath white sheets. He was dying all around her once again, and he was asking Dree why she had done it. Why she had left him.

But now that she was out of the waiting room, there was only one thought on her mind—the same one she'd had as they rushed Olli to the hospital: Was her family okay? She had to get home and check on them—now.

Dree turned to Marcus, who was still staring out at the city, dazed. The sun had risen hot and full to the south, melting the clouds away and leaving only a cobalt sky stained with the last remnants of smoke. It would have been beautiful, if not for the ruins below. She wondered again about Marcus. What did he know about these weapons?

"Listen, I really need to get home," Dree said. "What are you going to do?"

Marcus hesitated. He was still very shaken up, his eyes involuntarily darting back to the injured civilians and the crumbling homes. He still felt like he was going to faint every time he saw a white blanket laid across the ground. He shook his head.

"I don't know."

It was true enough. He'd had the desperate dream that he would go through the storm, find his father, and bring him home. Together, they would clear his name and rebuild their broken family. But he had no idea where to find his father in all this. The city was massive, and it was burning.

Dree didn't exactly need a companion, but she couldn't just leave Marcus wandering around the panicked city streets. He looked so lost, and more importantly, he seemed to know something about the machines. If Marcus had any information, she wanted to keep him close by.

"You can come with me," she said. "Then I can help you find . . . whatever it is you're looking for."

Marcus smiled. "Thanks."

They met eyes for just a moment, and Dree felt a very unexpected shiver run down the nape of her neck, tingling right through her spine and into her feet. She took a small step away from Marcus, she was so surprised.

Marcus had felt something too, and he was just as surprised. He'd never had that kind of jarring sensation before. He wasn't even sure what it was—it had been like a visceral shock to his bones. Not attraction, but like he was remembering something.

Dree quickly looked away. "Let's move."

The two of them cut through the city, with Dree slowing down just slightly to allow Marcus to keep up. Her athletic body was honed from years of hard labor in the forge, whereas Marcus had spent most of his time on a laptop drinking cola and eating chips. He was already nursing a cramp as he followed her down the street, weaving in and out of the crowd. People were bustling in all directions, harried and panicked.

As they ran, Marcus took out his phone again to check for progress. He was running the GPS search constantly, trying to grasp onto any faint signal. It was a vain hope, but since he hadn't actually traveled anywhere geographically, he was kind of hoping this world existed parallel to Arlington and that the signals might sneak through the same portal he had. But so far there was nothing. He was just a solitary blue dot on an empty space, which sort of reflected how he felt. He tried a call to Jack's cell phone.

No connection.

For years, Marcus's only focus had been to find his dad. That had taken up his entire adolescent life. It wasn't just that he wanted his dad back—though that of course was part of it—it was also that he couldn't bear to have his dad's reputation be that of a traitor. A spy. A disappointment to everyone—so much so that no one ever even sent Marcus a card after the disappearance. No one sent flowers. Even his brusque but proud grandpa, George's own father, refused to honor his son. Marcus had overheard him talking to Jack.

"If he's alive, he better not show his face near me ever again," his grandpa had spat. "A traitor . . . my own flesh and blood. It makes me sick."

Marcus cried for hours after he'd heard that, but he had never for a moment entertained the idea that his grandfather and the others were right. His father was a good man, and if

Marcus stopped searching for him, it would be like he finally believed the story.

He would have finally turned on his dad just like everybody else.

Maybe getting to this world proved that his dad hadn't taken off for Russia, but at what cost? He had led the drones to the portal, and they had subsequently destroyed an entire neighbourhood and killed hundreds. He never should have gone after that portal while he was under surveillance. He'd led the drones right to Dracone, and now whoever his father's enemies were, they were here too.

"What is that thing?" Dree asked, glancing back at him.

"My cell phone," he said distractedly. "Do you have phones?"

"Not that I know of," she replied. "Is it a weapon?"

Marcus snorted. "Not quite. Though it can do plenty of damage."

"I see," Dree said, not understanding at all.

They reached the docks, and Dree spotted her house, which was sitting untouched in the clump of decrepit old shacks. Relief flooded through her. Many of the other dockside homes weren't so lucky: She saw a few houses on fire and a couple more that had been completely leveled to pulp and ash. Obviously the machines had split up after the first pass on the city, as the destruction was widespread. From what she had seen, even one of those massive white ones could have leveled the entire docks by itself. It wouldn't take much to decimate the rickety old shacks.

She sprinted to her front door and threw it open.

"Abi? Dad?" She looked around. There was no one there. "Anyone?"

Fear gripped her like a cold hand wrapped around her throat. She frantically checked the small house, peeking in bedrooms and shouting their names over and over again. When she confirmed the house was abandoned, she hurried outside, almost bowling Marcus over as he stared down at his phone, frowning. He looked up anxiously.

"Are they okay?" he asked.

"They're not here," she said, looking through the window of her neighbors' house. They were gone too.

"Where are they?" she asked desperately, feeling anger and fear bubbling up beneath her skin like the burning embers in the forge. The fire was waiting. Just like that day with Gavri.

She couldn't stop it. She felt the heat rising, and she stepped away from Marcus.

"Dree?" a familiar voice said, and she turned to see old Mrs. Warmen emerge from her house, clothed in dirty brown rags, her silver hair a mess of knots. But she was a sharp old lady, and Dree had always liked her. "You're back."

"Where are they?" Dree asked instantly, running over and leaving Marcus behind.

"They left," she replied, her voice a hoarse croak. "Almost immediately after the fighting started. Your dad hustled them all out of there. He was headed for the school, I think—a lot of people took refuge there. Might be your best bet."

"Thank you," Dree said, relieved. "Are you all right?"

Mrs. Warmen waved a frail hand in dismissal. "I'm fine. I've lived through more dragon attacks than I care to count. Getting used to it. Not sure what those things were though . . . never seen anything like it."

"I know," Dree said. "I just hope they don't come back."

She thanked Mrs. Warmen again and returned to Marcus, who was still madly swiping his finger across the screen. Dree snuck a quick peek at the phone and saw words and numbers glowing through the glass, responding to every touch of his index finger.

"Where did you say you were from again?" she asked.

"Arlington."

Dree frowned. "Where's that?"

He lowered the phone. "That's what I was trying to find out. I have no idea."

"You don't know where your home is?"

Marcus shook his head. "No clue. My guess is it's far away, and that it won't be easy to get back to." He looked out over the city. "And I need to find my father."

Dree rubbed her forehead. "Now you're missing your father?"

Marcus nodded, cleaning the soot off his glasses. "I think he's here, in Dracone. But I have no idea where." He put his glasses back on. "What do we do now? Did she say your family was at a school? Want to go there?"

Dree thought about that for a moment. She knew her family was fine now; her dad would have Abi and the boys, and her mother was far away from the battle zone at the steel mill. Her mom would go to the docks and then head to the school as well.

The people she cares most about will all be there, Dree thought.

In truth, Dree didn't really know *how* her mother felt about her. But their relationship had definitely been strained over the years. When Dree was nine, her mother came into her bedroom late at night, as Dree had been tossing and turning her sleep. Rochin had already left to sleep in the main room.

She woke to her mother sitting beside her, the lines of her face glowing in the moonlight, her sad eyes watching Dree without sympathy or love. They looked cold.

"Was I shouting?" Dree asked quietly.

"Yes," she said. "You were saying his name."

Dree felt the sweat on her brow, the tears on her cheeks. "I'm sorry."

"You said that too," she murmured. "You said you were sorry to him. Why?"

Dree lay there silently. "Because I didn't save him."

Her eyes scanned over Dree.

"Is that all?"

Her mother suspected. Even at nine, Dree knew that. She saw her mother's whispered conversations with her father, she'd heard her parents yelling. Rochin didn't have nightmares. Or Abi.

It was only Dree.

"Yes," Dree whispered.

Her mother stared at her for a while and then patted her arm. "Go back to sleep."

She left without a word, but the coldness remained in the room. It wasn't always like that, though. Dree's mother still cooked for her and hugged her before work and washed her clothes.

But there were many other times when Dree was sure her mother hated her.

She shook the thought away. *What now?*

Dree could go and join her family, and she was desperate to check on Abi. But if the machines returned, even the squat, red-brick school would offer no protection. She had seen firsthand what their weapons could do. There would be no hiding from the machines in the city. If they were still somewhere nearby, they needed to be destroyed so that they couldn't return and hurt anyone else.

"No," Dree said quietly, "I need to go see a friend."

Chapter
11

"Why do you say *friend* so ominously?" Marcus asked, lowering his phone.

Dree shifted, not meeting his gaze. She was unlike any girl Marcus had ever met—pretty features but hard eyes, cold and aloof and yet bursting with fire. There was something else about her, though, and it had nothing to do with her appearance. It was like he knew her from somewhere. It was impossible, clearly, but he couldn't shake the feeling.

"He's not . . . friendly to strangers," she said slowly, not willing to trust Marcus with too much information. "Which is why we have to part ways here. I'm sorry."

Marcus was taken aback by the sudden change. He had seen so many horrors in the past hour that he didn't really want to be left alone, especially since he blamed himself for all the destruction. He felt nauseated again, and more importantly, he felt angry.

"Are you going to find a way to stop the drones?" he asked.

"I'm going to try," Dree admitted. "But it's too dangerous—"

"I'm coming," he interrupted.

She frowned. "No, you're not. My friend doesn't like new people."

"Well, tell him to get over it. I want to help."

"Why?"

Marcus wondered if he should tell her the truth. He had a feeling that if Dree knew it was his fault the drones had just destroyed half her city, she would either leave him behind or kill him on the spot. Looking at her calloused hands, scorched almost black, he doubted that she would even break a sweat. Besides, he was increasingly certain that the drones were somehow related to his father's disappearance. If he was ever going to have a chance at finding his father, he would have to find the drones first. And that meant following Dree.

"Because it's the right thing to do," he said firmly.

Dree wasn't convinced. She imagined what Lourdvang would say if she showed up at his cave with this bizarre foreign boy. For one, she had never brought another human to see Lourdvang before. He was a secret from everyone, and she liked it that way. But things had changed, and she needed all the help she could get—even from Marcus. She looked him over as he fidgeted and quickly crossed his arms, trying to press them across his chest so they didn't look so skinny. Dree couldn't help but smirk.

"Fine," she muttered. "But if you get killed, it's your own fault." She turned and started for the downtown core. "There's something we have to get you first."

Marcus hurried to catch up with her long strides. "Is it a gun?"

Dree looked back at him, confused. "No. Is that what those weapons were called?"

"The drones are armed with them, yes," Marcus explained. "They fire bullets. We're going to need them."

"We have other weapons."

"Does your friend have the weapons?"

"He is the weapon," she said quietly, looking around. "Can I ask you something?"

"Sure."

She hesitated, still unsure if she should tell him. But there wasn't much choice.

"How do you feel about dragons?"

Marcus stared at her, waiting for her to laugh. Or at least smile. But there was just a burning intensity in her blue eyes that didn't wane for a moment. She wasn't joking.

"I think they're cool. . . ." he said hesitantly, not sure what she was getting at.

"Why would they be cool?" Dree asked, confused.

"I mean I like them."

"Oh. Good." She looked both ways. "My friend . . . he's kind of a dragon."

"Like . . . a real one?" Marcus asked, lowering his voice.

"Yes. His name is Lourdvang. I found him when he was an infant."

Marcus tried to make sense of this new information. Considering he was in some sort of fantasy alter-world, it shouldn't have been surprising that there were dragons. But the logical part of his mind was still trying to catch up with all this, and dragons were just a bit much.

Of course, so was everything in Dracone. As they left the decimated south end, a full, breathing city materialized around him. His eyes fell on bizarre horned red birds perched on flagstone roofs, lizards on leashes like dogs, and wooden stands with all kinds of odd things for sale: fangs and eyes and organs. Ancient structures stood next to rudimentary steel buildings, matching the disparity in the people: peasant to beggar to garishly dressed aristocrats. It seemed that Dracone itself was caught between two worlds.

"Is that . . . normal? To have a dragon?" he asked.

Dree laughed for the first time since they'd met. It was surprisingly warm, like running water, and briefly distracted from the harshness in her eyes. "Of course not. You really are from far away, aren't you? Do you know anything about dragons?"

"Not really."

Dree sighed. She figured now was as good of a time as ever to explain Dracone's history with dragons to Marcus.

"Ten years ago, it may have been considered somewhat

normal to have a dragon. Humans and dragons . . . we co-existed peacefully. Some dragons were even close friends, particularly the Nightwings and Sages. Dragon riders protected the kingdom and kept the peace. They were men and women chosen as kids—usually ten years old—to face the dragon elders. If they were deemed worthy, they would be allowed to meet dragon youths. If a bond was made between a human and a dragon, they trained together for many years to become warriors. They protected Dracone from wild dragons and attackers from the east, and they were symbols of hope. There were incidents between humans and dragons, of course . . . Outliers are wild and sometimes attacked humans, and if a Flame ever came down from the Teeth, entire villages could be destroyed. But that was very rare, and for the most part, we lived in peace."

Marcus nodded, though some of the story made no sense to him. He didn't want Dree to stop talking, though.

"So what happened?" Marcus asked, watching a soot-covered child run past. He hoped the boy's family was nearby—he didn't want to think that he could be an orphan.

"We changed, I guess. There was an attack once, by the Flames. They burned a village called Toloth to the ground, and public opinion turned against the dragons. The newly elected prime minister, Francis Xidorne, was especially angry. Apparently he had a close friend there, a scientist who had helped design many of the new technologies that Francis was promoting. Most of his platform was about advancing Dracone into a new age, and when his friend was killed in the attack, it ruined his plans. So he instituted new laws banning humans and dragons from interacting. He started the hunts, and humans started to shoot Outliers down from the sky. Once a human killed a Sage—the kindest and most peaceful of the dragons— the lines of war were set. The dragons turned their backs on us. Even the Nightwings, our closest friends."

"And the riders?" Marcus asked.

"Branded traitors," Dree said bitterly. "Stripped of their fortunes and forbidden from seeing even their own dragons. The penalty for befriending or helping a dragon is still death. My father was a dragon rider. . . . He was never the same after."

She paused.

"I was seven when I found Lourdvang. Even then, I knew the rule about dragons, but I couldn't leave him. He was scared, and so small. The hunters would have killed him, or he would have died of starvation. So I raised him in a little hidden cave outside the city, and as he grew, we became very close. I still see him as much as I can."

Marcus rubbed his forehead, bewildered. Something occurred to him.

"So what do we need to get?" he asked.

Dree looked at him. "Armor."

⊕

A few minutes later they were staring at a little smithy with an old wooden sign reading WILHELM'S FORGE. It was tucked onto the side of a busy street, still bustling with the strange array of people. The attacks had been far enough from the city center that people there were largely continuing with their daily routine. Marcus focused on the strangely dressed ones—they were wearing everything from gleaming black armor to sleeveless shirts to suits, all adorned with fang necklaces and earrings and other unusual accessories. Their faces were even weirder: eyebrows shaved or scorched off, strange tattoos, and hair that was buzzed or shaved into Mohawks.

"What's with the punk rockers?" he whispered.

"The what?"

"The weird ones," he said.

Dree scowled. "It's the new trend," she muttered. "Killing dragons became a symbol of the new Dracone, and so people started buying fangs and scales. The hairstyles and eyebrows and everything else followed. It's all supposed to symbolize a mastery of fire. Fire was the age-old enemy of humans when dragons attacked, so mastering it is supposedly a sign of our progress."

Dree seemed to be getting angry, so Marcus decided to change the subject.

"So what are we doing here again?"

Dree suddenly cut into the crowd. "Borrowing armor."

As they crossed the street, Marcus noticed a lot of people giving him very curious glances. Some looked confused, others alarmed, and some of the young people with the crimson Mohawks and shaved heads almost looked like they admired Marcus, like he was on the cusp of some new fashion statement. They were pointing at his clothes and whispering to one another, smiling and giving him approving nods like he had done something clever. He felt uncomfortable with so many eyes on him. Maybe he needed to find some new clothes. Dree didn't even notice; she was focused on the shop.

They cut through an alley that ran beside the forge and emerged onto a dingy backstreet where there were far fewer wealthy young Draconians and more people begging in the corners, nothing but crumpled robes and frail, grasping hands. It was the other side of Dracone—so close to the shiny exterior. The forgotten underclass.

Dree led him to a small back door with a massive iron padlock.

Marcus frowned when he saw it. "How are we going to—"

Before he could even finish, Dree withdrew a slender piece of metal from her pack and started picking the lock. It didn't take long. Her fingers were deft and clever, and in a few seconds the padlock popped open. Marcus looked at her, raising his eyebrows.

"I made it," she said simply.

Easing the door open, Dree put a finger to her lips and crept into the shadows. It was morning, and Sasha would already be working in the forge. Master Wilhelm was probably helping, unless he had managed to find himself a new apprentice already. Wilhelm wasn't the type to close the forge for a day, even if the city was under attack. Especially since they were making weapons—if anything, they would be working longer hours to meet what surely would be increased demand.

Marcus took an anxious look around the backstreet and followed Dree inside. He wasn't sure he wanted to be caught stealing. . . . The penalty could be cutting off his hand or something. He swung the door shut behind him, noticing a beggar staring.

As usual, the inside of the forge was scorching hot and stained with soot, like the inside of a coal-fired barbecue. Marcus's eyes stung against the pressing heat, and he could just make out Dree as she quietly snuck through the hallway and into a side room. Up ahead he saw an orange glow and a large silhouette. Someone was working.

Marcus nervously followed Dree into the room and realized it was an armory.

Racks of swords and spears and jousts lined the blackened walls, while shields and armor hung between them. Great crossbows and lances sat in the corner along with steel arrows that were three feet long and barbed. It was an impressive collection, but Dree knew exactly what she wanted. She hurried straight to a chainmail, ebony outfit on the far wall. Grabbing it off the rack, she gestured for Marcus to put it on.

"What is it?" he asked, eyeing the strange material.

"Fire-resistant armor," she said. "You'll need it to ride Lourdvang."

"Where's yours?"

"I don't need it. Now hurry up!" She turned around to give him privacy.

Marcus hesitated and then quickly took off his pants

and shirt, sliding the strange black outfit over his boxers. It was made of hard steel, warmed up in the heat of the shop, but it was oddly light and flexible, like a fine mesh. There was a shirt to slide on and matching ebony pants, and once they were on, he put his jeans and T-shirt over them. There were matching gloves as well, and he shoved those into his pockets.

"Okay."

Dree turned around and looked over him, nodding. "How does it feel?"

"Weird," he said. "Very light."

She grinned. "Of course. I made it. Now let's get out of here before—"

They were too late. They heard heavy footsteps and turned to see Sasha walk into the armory, sweating as he lugged a clump of freshly forged swords. Sasha's jaw dropped when he saw them, and almost instantly, his furious gaze jumped to the exorbitantly priced, fire-resistant armor that was exposed on Marcus's arms, and the empty spot where it had been hanging on the wall.

Dree knew exactly what Sasha was thinking. And they were in trouble.

"What is this—" he started.

"It's not what it looks like, Sasha," Dree said, moving toward him. "We just need to borrow the armor. The city is under attack, and we need to stop the drones before—"

He scowled. "Nice try. You're going to sell this on the street. I don't think so, Dree. Tonin!" he called down the hall. "Come here!" Sasha turned back to Dree and smirked.

"Your replacement. He knows how to actually do the job, which is a nice change. Let's go—we're taking you two to Wilhelm. He might take a hand for this."

Marcus blanched. The boy was huge—they'd never get past him.

"Fine," Dree said, putting her head down. "Take us."

Marcus was about to argue that maybe they were giving in a little too easily, when suddenly Dree thrust her knee hard into Sasha's groin, who swore and dropped the pile of swords. Before Sasha could react, Dree punched him across the face, sending him toppling backward to the floor. Dree's fist throbbed as she turned back to Marcus.

"Run!"

Marcus quickly followed her down the hall and back into the blinding daylight, still stunned by her unexpected attack. But Sasha was quick to recover. He and Tonin burst from the forge behind them, both wielding swords, Sasha looking murderous.

"We're heading for the mountains!" Dree shouted to Marcus. "Stay close."

"Yeah," Marcus managed, trying to keep up and already feeling his sides burning with cramps. "How far are the mountains?"

"Just run!"

Marcus took a look back and saw that the two barrel-chested boys were closing in. They looked like defensive tackles. He was just turning back to Dree when his left foot hit an exposed edge in the cobblestone. Pain flared through his big toe and he went flying forward, crashing into the road and skidding along the weathered gray stones.

He groaned and rolled over onto his back.

Dree slid to a halt and turned around, cursing. Sasha was closing in fast, and she remembered his violent temper: He might just cut them both into ribbons without thinking. She sprinted back to Marcus and yanked him up, knowing that she was too late. Sasha was already lifting the broadsword before them. He looked crazed.

Dree was preparing to push Marcus out of the way when Sasha and Tonin abruptly dropped their swords, as an enormous winged shadow fell across the street. Marcus slowly turned around, feeling all the hairs on the back of his neck stand up.

There, swooping to a landing directly behind them, was Lourdvang.

The heat swept through Marcus again, and he took a step back, raising his hands in terror. The color drained from his cheeks. The dragon was enormous—as big as a two-story house and nothing but black scales and claws and teeth the size of Marcus's forearm.

Lourdvang took up half the street, blocking the sun completely until his huge, membranous wings curled up onto his back. The beggars all disappeared into the shadows, shouting warnings. Marcus was tempted to join them. His knees shook.

Dree looked up in shock. "Lourdvang? What are you doing here?"

"The enemy is returning," he growled. "You must flee."

Marcus's fear was momentarily replaced by wonder. *The dragons can speak?*

Dree looked at Marcus. "Can he come? He has the armor."

Lourdvang looked at Marcus and paused, his flashing cobalt eyes narrowing into something almost catlike. His teeth were still exposed, and Marcus had the very distinct sensation that the dragon didn't like him. He took another tiny step backward.

"Lourdvang," Dree said, sounding like a reprimanding parent.

"Fine," he grumbled. "Hurry up."

Marcus slipped on his mesh gloves and very hesitantly followed Dree onto the massive dragon's back, using the angled black scales as handholds. Dree sat right at the base of Lourdvang's neck, and Marcus slid behind her, looking around awkwardly for something to grab.

"Around my waist," she ordered.

Marcus flushed and quickly wrapped his arms around her waist. Her stomach was very hard and lined with muscle, tensing as she gripped the scales and leaned forward.

"Hold on tight," Dree said.

"Okay," Marcus murmured, barely trusting himself to speak.

He glanced down at Sasha and Tonin, who were both still looking on in shock, and then saw a group of heavily armed soldiers in black armor turn onto the street ahead, raising their swords and spears and shouting war cries.

"Now!" Dree shouted.

Lourdvang leapt into the air, and Marcus could barely hold on to Dree as Lourdvang's wings unfurled and swept downward, sending them shooting toward the sky. Almost simultaneously, they heard a now familiar noise: the rapid thunder of machine guns. Behind Lourdvang, an arrow point of three white drones swept across the city, firing indiscriminately once again. Lourdvang angled sharply to the east, beating his massive wings faster now, and he had just wheeled off the side street as the machine guns leapt across it, shattering the cobblestone road and gunning down civilians.

Marcus thought he saw Sasha and Tonin go down, and the nausea rose again, but he didn't have much time to think about it. Lourdvang accelerated rapidly, heading toward the waiting mountains. Marcus clutched Dree as the city shrunk away beneath them. They were ascending almost straight up, and Marcus felt like if he let go he might plummet right off the dragon's back. He tightened his grip on Dree's waist.

And then, to his surprise, he felt his lips curl in an unbidden smile.

When Lourdvang was high enough, he opened his great wings fully and glided on the breeze, heading for the mountains that stretched out into the eastern horizon like cresting waves. Marcus shouted in fear as Lourdvang suddenly lost altitude, following the current, and then broke out laughing as Lourdvang dropped again and rose just as sharply, the cold wind beating past Marcus's face. For a moment, he felt completely free. All his awkwardness and clumsiness on the ground were gone up in the sky, swept away in a graceful dance on the current. Despite the horrors below, Marcus felt more alive than he'd felt in his entire life, and a desperate euphoria swept through him. In that moment, Marcus had a thought that really made no sense at all: Maybe he belonged here, in this world. Maybe he belonged on a dragon.

And then he took a look back.

Behind them, the city was burning. Black smoke was already billowing into the sky from multiple locations, and fires were leaping up everywhere. Another building collapsed, shooting a cloud of dust through the city streets. It was chaos.

Marcus's joy instantly dissolved into guilt and fear. For the moment, the search for his father could wait. . . . He had a new mission.

He was going to find some way to destroy those drones.

Chapter 12

As they closed in on the first enormous mountain to the east, its snowcapped peak catching the sun, Marcus loosened his grip on Dree's waist and slid back, giving her more space. They had been pressed tightly together for the past few minutes, warming them against the cold wind. Dree relaxed a little, dropping her shoulders and her guard. No one had ever held her that long, and she wasn't comfortable being touched. It wasn't safe.

Marcus was just as uncomfortable holding her, and he let his hands rest awkwardly on her hips instead. He could still catch her scent on the wind though. It was like the dying embers of his old fireplace—a smoky, comforting scent that reminded him of his father. Despite that, his mind was preoccupied with another matter. He had realized that there was something strangely *right* about being up in the air. But how was that possible? How was he so comfortable on the back of a dragon?

He felt himself swaying in rhythm with Lourdvang as the dragon swept up and down on the invisible currents, sometimes wheeling in either direction to catch a howling gust and accelerate. Marcus considered the physics of what was happening: the huge membranous wings that tilted by mere inches to elevate or descend, the twenty-foot-long tail angling like a propeller, and the four powerful legs tucked against his broad chest for increased aerodynamics and speed. It was flying in the most natural way possible.

"This is awesome," Marcus said, shaking his head in wonder.

Dree looked back and smiled. "This is my favorite place in the world."

She looked different up there. Happy. Marcus flushed again and turned back to the wings, pointing with a black-gloved hand while the other remained loosely on her hip.

"It's amazing how Lourdvang's wings are so flexible," he called over the wind. "They're almost on fully rotational joints, so he can stop and turn instantly. And the width of them . . . they pick up the current so easily, and he barely has to move them."

Dree looked at Marcus as he continued, a frown line creeping down between her eyes. Marcus had claimed he didn't know anything about dragons, but he was describing their flight mechanics very accurately.

"Of course, he must be incredibly heavy with these armor-plated scales, so it still seems almost impossible that he can fly." Marcus paused. "I wonder if the fire is somehow helping, like a blimp. Either way, I'm guessing even a decent-sized hole in one of those wings would disrupt the entire system. In fact, I doubt he could fly at all if one of his wings was punctured even a foot in diameter. The system is too dependent on a steady, uninterrupted airflow, and he's too heavy to compensate."

Lourdvang arched his neck and turned back, giving Marcus a suspicious look.

"Who is this . . . boy, Dree?" he asked, sounding a bit threatening.

Marcus shrunk back behind Dree a little. He didn't like those teeth.

"A friend," Dree said, patting Lourdvang's neck. "We just met."

Lourdvang snorted and turned back, twin plumes of smoke trailing out of his nostrils. "So he's a stranger. A weird one at that."

"We're working on his people skills," Dree whispered to Marcus.

Marcus frowned. "I see. I get the impression he doesn't like me."

"He doesn't," Lourdvang confirmed.

Dree sighed. "He's just a little protective. Even though he's the younger one," she said, elevating her voice to make sure Lourdvang could hear her. She turned to face Marcus fully.

Dree already knew a lot of what Marcus had described, both from what she observed in Lourdvang and from what she'd been taught at the forge by Master Wilhelm. Understanding how a dragon flew was vital in learning how to bring it down. It was why the metal projectiles in the city's catapults were about a foot around and very sharp—so that they could cut through the wing membranes. It was also why the arrows in the oversized crossbows in the guard towers had jagged barbs and hooks, to tear on their way through the wings.

It was extremely cruel, but it was the only way to bring a dragon down.

"How do you know all that stuff about how dragons fly?"

Marcus shrugged. "It's just basic physics."

"We learned about the wings in the forge," she said softly. "When they were teaching us how to kill dragons."

Lourdvang growled. Marcus felt his entire body vibrate.

"Why would you want to do that?" Marcus asked.

Dree's eyes narrowed. "I didn't. But like I said, hunting dragons is big business these days. We made weapons to kill dragons."

"Doesn't that seem a little contradictory for you?"

"Yes," Lourdvang growled.

"I tried to avoid making them," she explained. "And trust me, I didn't show them half of the weapons I could have created." She hesitated. "Pretend you didn't hear that."

Marcus laughed. "Who would I tell?"

The first mountain passed below them, and Dree frowned. She had assumed they would go to Lourdvang's hidden cave to regroup and think of a strategy.

"Where are we going?" Dree called to Lourdvang.

"To see my clan."

"Is that a good idea?" she asked, her voice a bit shaky.

Dree had never been to the Nightwings' lair, Forost, for obvious reasons. Humans were not welcome there, and Lourdvang wouldn't be either if the Nightwings knew about his friendship with Dree.

Lourdvang snorted. "Probably not. But we have to act. Those machines already hit the mountains and shot down a Nightwing. They have brought the war to us, which is why I came to find you. Things have changed."

They were flying along the edge of the mountains, and Marcus saw some scattered towns and farmhouses in the sprawling plains to the right, tucked into the valley and lined with roads and wheat fields and ambling carts. It was a beautiful place . . . serene and brimming with life.

"Are there cities out there?" He looked out to where sky met earth in the distance.

"Yes," Dree said. "Dracone is the capitol of Errenia, our state. It's the greatest city. But there are smaller ones in Errenia, and outside of that, only the dragons know. We don't leave Errenia."

"A wise choice," Lourdvang said. "I have flown over other lands. Dragons live there, and so do other creatures . . . dangerous ones. Just hope you never find yourself there."

"So what are we going to do?" Marcus asked, as Lourdvang started angling into the mountain range, his wings adjusting to the current to send them into a graceful turn.

"Dree and I are going to try to convince my clan to fight with us," Lourdvang said. "If the Nightwings agree to attack the machines, we may have a chance. *You* are going to stand there quietly and try not to be eaten."

"Their wings will be very vulnerable to bullets," Marcus warned.

"We know how to fight," Lourdvang rumbled. "We use our bodies to shield our wings. I doubt their weapons can pierce my scales."

Marcus considered that. "They could be armor piercing." He slipped one of his gloves off and went to touch the scales beside him. "What are they made out of—"

Dree quickly grabbed his arm. "Don't touch!" she snapped. "They're very hot. Why do you think we stole you that armor?"

She released his hand and turned away. Her father had told her once that humans used to burn themselves constantly on dragon scales when the two species were friends. The fact that Dree could touch them without gloves or armor was just another sign of the fire within her. Even her father didn't have that ability. He had always worn armor.

"Why doesn't it burn you?" Marcus asked.

Dree hesitated. "It just doesn't."

Marcus knew he should listen to Dree's warning, but he couldn't resist. As soon as she turned away from him, he quickly touched the scales. They felt warm, but they certainly weren't scalding. Making sure Dree wasn't watching, he laid his right hand fully on Lourdvang's back, feeling the warmth spill into his fingers. Dree glanced at him.

Her eyes widened. "How are you doing that?"

"It's not even hot," he said, showing Dree his hand. "See?"

Dree took Marcus's hand, examining every inch of it. His fingers should have been covered in painful blisters, yet they were completely smooth. She slowly ran her thumb across his palm, wondering why it wasn't even the slightest bit burned.

Dree suddenly realized what she was doing and dropped his hand, spotting the awkward look on Marcus's face.

"Sorry," she murmured. "I've just never met anyone else who can do that."

Marcus shrugged. "Does that mean I can take this armor off?"

"I would keep it on if I were you," Lourdvang grumbled, as they started a rapid descent toward a huge, stout mountain so pockmarked with caves that it looked like a beehive. The top was marked with a shallow cap of white snow, and a few straggly trees and shrubs lined the steep, rocky slopes. Far below, a river cut through the valley.

"What is this place?" Marcus shouted.

"Forost—the home of the Nightwings," Dree said. "And they don't like humans."

Lourdvang swept onto an exposed ledge, landing with a

final flap of his wings and settling gracefully onto the stone. Marcus saw eyes watching them from many of the dark caves, and they had just climbed off Lourdvang's back when two black dragons emerged from a large opening ahead, smoke already curling from their mouths.

"What is this?" one of them, a burly dragon with a thick midsection, rumbled. "Do you ask for death?"

Lourdvang stepped in the way. "I would like to speak with Erdath."

The two dragons scoffed.

"Even he won't forgive you for this, Lourdvang," the first dragon said. "He has cut you enough slack already. You will face exile for this. Hopefully death."

Marcus scanned the mountainside but saw no way they could escape. They were way too exposed out on the ledge, hundreds of feet above the valley. If the Nightwings attacked them, they would most certainly die.

Lourdvang snarled and stepped toward the two dragons.

"Try it," he said, baring his teeth.

The two dragons prepared to launch themselves, and Marcus was just about to grab Dree and dive onto the ground when a third dragon emerged from the darkness.

"Control yourselves," the new dragon said, his deep voice rumbling the entire mountain. The dragon's skin was a steely onyx, and he was seemingly older than the others, with a wrinkled face and scars and pockmarks on his scales. But though he may have looked older, his eyes—as green as the valley below, with slitlike pupils—were sharp and cunning.

"Erdath," Lourdvang said, "I have brought these humans because they too are under attack, and they know more about these machines than we do. They can help us."

Erdath's eyes fell on Dree and Marcus. Dree fidgeted, wondering if the elder would agree to hear them out. If he didn't, they were dead.

Finally, Erdath nodded and turned back to the cavern.

"You may enter. And for all our sakes, I hope Lourdvang is right."

Chapter

13

Dree looked around in wonder as they followed Lourdvang into Forost, a place that no human had set foot in for over a decade. It was brighter than the Flames' lair, as multiple tunnels to the surface let pale daylight spill into the cavern. Dragons didn't need furniture or care much for decor, so it too was just barren stone, but everything felt a little less ominous, if only because she felt far safer with Nightwings.

Still, Dree and Marcus could feel dozens of eyes on them as they walked into the cavern, where a large crowd of dragons had already gathered. They glared at the humans as they walked by, and Dree heard many of the dragons muttering in their language. She knew the ones at the gate had spoken the human tongue only so Marcus and Dree could understand them and be suitably afraid. Mostly, when dragons talked to one another, they stuck to their own language. Grumbles and hisses and snorts filled the room as the creatures conversed.

Erdath stepped onto a raised stone dais—much like the one Helvath had been perched upon, though thankfully not made of bones—and looked down at them. Marcus couldn't be sure, but he thought that Erdath seemed sad as he stared at Dree and Marcus. He looked like a wizened old man.

"It has been a long time since a human stood before me," he said.

Dree bowed her head. "That is the fault of my people."

"You're right," he agreed. "But it is the sadness of mine."

Dree felt a sharp stab of guilt. Humans had turned against the dragons, not the other way around. They had expanded into dragon territory, they had hunted them like deer, and then, to add to the insult, they had worn their fangs and scales like jewelry. Humans had turned on their ancient friends, and they had done so swiftly and without apology.

"Tell me," Erdath said, "what are these things that have taken over our skies?"

Dree opened her mouth to speak, but Marcus beat her to it. He had been looking around the room in awe, amazed at the assembly of dragons. This was a community of sentient, intelligent beings, which made the fact that he had seen their body parts for sale in the city all the more disturbing.

"They're called drones," he said.

Lourdvang turned to Marcus, his eyes narrowing again.

"Drones?" Erdath asked.

Marcus nodded. "They're automated machines, meaning there are no people inside of them. They can be controlled from anywhere, and they are very dangerous. They have heavy armor, air-to-surface missiles, and dual machine guns." Erdath tilted his head in confusion. "Guns . . . they're weapons that shoot tiny pointed pieces of metal. The metal looks invisible because it moves so quickly, but guns are extremely deadly."

"How do you know all of this?" Erdath asked.

"Because they come from the same place I do," Marcus said, shifting his eyes to the ground. "The United States. I've seen them before. Well, the one kind with the red eyes, anyway. But I don't know what they want or why they're attacking Dracone. It doesn't make any sense."

Dree stared at him, scowling. Marcus had never mentioned that he'd seen the drones before.

"These machines have killed one of my kin already," Erdath growled.

"And hundreds of mine," Dree said, looking up at the ancient dragon. "That's why we've come. We want to find a way to destroy them, and we need your help."

"How do you know Lourdvang?" Erdath asked suddenly, as if the thought had only just occurred to him.

Lourdvang shifted, and Dree spoke before he could say anything. "He saved our lives. We were under attack in the city, and he swooped down and saved us."

"Is this true?" Erdath asked, turning to Lourdvang.

"It is," Lourdvang said, not meeting Erdath's eyes.

Erdath watched him for a moment, and then looked at Dree. "And what do you want from us?"

"Help. We want you to attack the drones and destroy them."

"I see," he replied softly.

Erdath looked out over the assembled dragons, and Marcus watched as he seemed to consider each one individually.

Finally, he spoke. "We cannot help you."

Dree started and turned to Lourdvang, who looked surprised.

"Why not?" Lourdvang demanded.

"Because I believe these drones are after the humans," Erdath said calmly. "The dragon that was killed was flying near a human settlement. I don't think he was targeted. You say the drones have killed hundreds of humans, and I doubt the attacks are done. I have ordered all my clan to remain in the mountain until these drones leave Dracone."

He met Dree's eyes, looking sad.

"Once I might have risked our clan to help humans— once they were our brothers and sisters. But those days are long past, lost in the memories of my dead kin. We will not punish you for asking, and you may leave this place unharmed, but we will not help you. If the drones wipe out your people, I will weep for them, but my children will be safer. Take shelter for now, if you wish, and make your plans. If Lourdvang wants to help you, so be it."

✛

Dree sat perched against Lourdvang's stomach, feeling his familiar heat running through her. They were sitting in a shadowy corner of the main cavern, partially hidden from the scrutinizing eyes of the others. They had decided to stay there for the moment, until they could come up with some sort of plan. But no matter how hard Dree tried, she couldn't see a way to defeat the machines without the help of the Nightwings. Even with Lourdvang by their side, they were outmatched—and there was no one else to turn to.

The Outliers would attack on sight if Dree and Marcus went to their lair, and the Sages wouldn't fight even if Dree could find them. The Flames, of course, weren't an option—they'd sooner die than help the humans or another dragon clan.

Dree watched as Marcus paced back and forth, wringing his hands and muttering to himself. He had spoken very little since they had gotten to the cavern, and he kept checking his phone.

Marcus just kept mumbling questions.

"But how can the remote transmitter be reaching them?"

"Can the drones cross back and forth through the portal?"

"Is there some way to block the signal?"

Dree was busy wondering if her family was all right. It had killed her to leave the city without checking on them, but she knew they would have nowhere to hide if the drones decided to level Dracone. Until the drones were destroyed, her family was in danger.

She had originally thought she could use Lourdvang to attack the drones, but having seen them in action a few times now, she knew that even Lourdvang didn't stand much chance against five drones. Marcus was right: They would tear his wings to ribbons.

"Have you made any more weapons?" Lourdvang asked her quietly.

She shook her head. "No. And without access to the forge, I can't make anything. Besides, I don't think any of my weapons would do much good against flying steel. My weapons were designed to fight soldiers—to protect you from lances and arrows and spears."

"Where did you meet this boy?" Lourdvang asked quietly, eyeing Marcus as he paced.

"The street. He appeared out of nowhere."

"Do you think he's connected to these drones?"

"I don't know," she admitted. "Maybe. But they tried to kill him like everyone else, and he seemed just as surprised to see them."

"I don't trust him."

"I know," Dree said. "But I don't think he's involved."

Lourdvang snorted, blowing out a cloud of black smoke.

Marcus was still marching around, muttering under his breath and adjusting his glasses. He was completely covered in soot, but he had wiped the glasses, and Dree could see his gray eyes scanning over the phone.

"Besides," Dree said. "I still think he's our best chance to figure out—"

Marcus suddenly froze, staring at something on the far wall. The cavern walls had looked barren at first glance, but he saw now that wasn't the case. There was something written on the stone near the entrance. Without another word, he sprinted over to the wall.

"I knew it," he whispered.

Dree and Lourdvang exchanged a look and then followed him over.

"What is it?" Dree asked, examining the numbers and letters on the wall.

Marcus just stared at them in silence, scanning over the complicated pattern. It was drawn with some sort of black clay—it must have taken hours of work. Marcus doubted it came from the dragons. There was no way they could write with their massive black claws. He wasn't even sure it was written by anyone in Dracone. The sequence of numbers, dashes, and semicolons . . . they could be only one thing: code. Someone had written an extremely complex programming code on the wall. He couldn't understand it, but it meant his suspicions had been confirmed. Someone from his world had been there.

And there, small at the bottom, was the symbol. Three rectangles, but no eyes. It was the same symbol that had been carved into his father's desk. Could it have been him?

"How long has this been here?" he asked, turning to Lourdvang.

"Many years," Lourdvang said. "Erdath told me that a human put it there. It's just nonsense."

"No," Marcus said softly, turning back to the wall and carefully running his hands over the numbers. "It's computer code. Programming."

Dree was confused. "Do you know what it means?"

"No," he said, "not yet."

Marcus removed his phone from his pocket and took a picture of the writing, the flash lighting up the cavern. He could plug the code into his laptop later and analyze it with HTML software.

"Did Erdath know the human's name? Did he ever tell you?"

"No," Lourdvang said. "The man never said his name. He came twice. The first time he came asking about the Egg, and when Erdath told him the Flames had it, he left. He returned a few years later and asked to leave this message here."

"The Egg?" Marcus asked.

"Ancient dragon magic," Dree replied. "A relic with terrible power."

Marcus turned back to the wall. Could this mysterious man really have been his father, or was it someone else? Someone who wanted Dracone's treasures.

He thought about the rolling green fields, the untapped mountain ranges, and the lake stretching off into the horizon. This world was probably full of resources: oil and gold and diamonds. Bizarre creatures and artifacts that could be priceless on Earth.

A new theory abruptly fell into place. One that explained the appearance of the drones and the vicious attacks on the city. He couldn't prove it yet, but it made an awful lot of sense.

Maybe whoever was controlling those drones didn't want Marcus. They wanted Dracone and the rest of this unspoiled world. The implications hit him right in the gut. His father might have figured it out. What if he had disappeared that day to *close* the portal?

If that was true, then Marcus had just undone his father's work. He met Dree's eyes, the grim truth finally revealing itself. It was even worse than he thought.

"I think I know why the drones are attacking," he said. "And if I'm right, they won't stop until every living thing in Dracone has been completely wiped out."

Chapter 14

Dree stared at Marcus, confused. "I don't understand. Who is attacking us?"

Marcus turned back to the code. He scanned over the numbers again, his lips moving with silent words. It was highly advanced programming—much more complicated than anything he had ever attempted. He used HTML to build websites and even to hack into media databases, looking for unpublished stories about his father's disappearance—but that was child's play compared with this. As far as he could tell, this code was layered with variable instructions and open-ended algorithms. It could deliver messages like any other, but it could also decide by itself the best way to fulfill its mission. It was highly advanced artificial intelligence, unusual and very complex. It also gave him a very strong indication of what this code was for.

"The place where I come from," Marcus said. "It's a country called the United States of America. My father worked for the government there."

"So?"

"So when my father disappeared eight years ago, he took off suddenly and never told me where he was going. Agents showed up the next day and said he was a spy and a traitor and all these terrible things that I never believed. Now I think I know why."

He gestured around them.

"The government already knew about Dracone. They'd already been here. And they found a new world full of resources and minerals . . . unclaimed. Everything is untapped here: gold, oil, diamonds, even water. It's priceless, and they can access it through a rift in space. Immeasurable resources . . . all available within their own borders."

Dree rubbed her forehead. "You're losing me."

"I think the U.S. government wants Dracone for itself. If they destroy all of Dracone's citizens and the dragons, they can take this entire world and use all of its resources. I believe my father found out about this and tried to stop them. He came here and tried to disrupt the storms—the portals to Dracone—but now the storms have started again, and the government has sent in the drones to wipe you all out."

The information was too much for Dree. So much of

it didn't make any sense, but there was one thing that had stood out to her.

"The drones came in a storm?"

Marcus nodded. "Yes. In my world a violent storm appears once every year. The date counted down, and on the final day the portal opened."

Dree narrowed her eyes. "You came in a storm."

Marcus stopped, shifting uncomfortably. He adjusted his glasses, refusing to meet her stone-faced gaze. Beside Dree, Lourdvang was watching in silence. He wondered how the enormous dragon would react. Hopefully not by eating him.

"Yes," he said softly. "I came in the same storm. They were chasing me in my world, and . . . I think they followed me through the portal."

Dree didn't even think. She just cocked her fist and punched Marcus right in the chin. He dropped, stunned by the unexpected blow. She stood over him, her fists balled and quivering. He had brought the drones here. He was responsible for the deaths of all those people. He had put her family in danger.

"I deserved that," Marcus managed, rubbing his chin. "But it wasn't my fault."

"You just said—"

"They followed me," he said weakly, looking up at her. "I don't think they knew how to find the portal. I didn't know. . . . I just rode into the center of the storm. I was trying to find my father."

Dree softened. Marcus's voice had a pleading tone to

it, and Dree could hear his terrible guilt. She understood searching for a father. She was always looking for hers—the proud man he used to be. She loosened her fists and stepped back, crossing her arms across her chest instead.

Marcus slowly pushed himself to his feet.

"I'm sorry," he said. "I never wanted this. I'll help you stop them."

"How?" she snarled, not ready to forgive him quite yet.

She had saved his life, dragging him through the streets of Dracone and even onto Lourdvang's back. All that time, he had known exactly what the drones were and where they had come from, but he hadn't been honest. He may not have orchestrated the attacks, but he was at least partly responsible for them.

Marcus hesitated. "I don't know yet. But I know what they're doing, and I believe this code may have something to do with it." He patted his bag. "I probably have another couple of days of power on my laptop if I leave it off, so we have to move quickly."

Dree was still reluctant, and she looked at Lourdvang. He stared at Marcus.

"Why should we trust you?" he asked.

"Because if I had anything to do with those drones, I could call them here right now and kill you all."

Dree and Marcus exchanged a resigned look.

"So we have to find the drones," Dree said.

Marcus nodded. "Yeah. But how to find them without being killed is the question." He met her eyes. "I am sorry, really."

Dree kind of wanted to hit him one more time, but she knew he was being sincere. And maybe he could help her stop the drones. It might be their only chance.

"Fine," she muttered. "But from now on you tell me the truth—"

She was interrupted as a Nightwing suddenly swept into the cavern, skidding to a halt in the center of the room. He was clearly young, half the size of Lourdvang and so black he looked like a living shadow. He also seemed agitated, hurrying toward the circular stone dais, which was currently empty. Erdath emerged from a back cavern.

"We were worried, Ralar," he rumbled. "You were gone too long."

Ralar replied in the rasping dragon tongue, and Dree and Marcus hurried over to see what was going on, followed by Lourdvang. Erdath glanced at them.

"Speak in the human tongue," he ordered.

Ralar seemed confused and then noticed Dree and Marcus for the first time. He started, stepping away from them and lowering his head menacingly.

"It's fine," Erdath said impatiently. "Speak."

The dragon looked reluctant but continued. "The machines do not tire. They travel the skies like a flock of fell birds. I have seen three different ones now: some with red eyes, black as night, that watch the cities; others small like sparrows, sweeping the countryside tirelessly; and others white as snow—bigger than the rest—that strike without warning and then vanish again."

Marcus listened, fascinated. There was a third type as well? Where were they coming from? Was the portal still open? If it was, they needed to close it. Soon.

"What have they attacked?" Erdath asked.

"Everything. Towns have crumbled. The city is hit again and again. I saw dragon hunters try to fight them with steel arrows and spears and hooks, but they were no use against the machines. They were all slain. Three Outliers stumbled across their path, and they were shot out of the sky. I heard them screaming."

Ralar shuddered, and a sick feeling settled into Dree's stomach. Erdath looked at her, guessing at her thoughts. "Is the city destroyed?"

"Some of it," Ralar said. "They have not hit the palace yet, nor much of the downtown area. So far it is mostly the outskirts. Even the children are not spared."

Dree's head popped up. "What do you mean?"

The dragon hesitated. "They attacked one of your schools. It burns even now."

Dree felt her knees buckle. She could barely speak.

"Was it near the lake?" she whispered.

The dragon nodded. "Yes. It burns right on the water."

"I'm coming with you," Marcus said, hurrying after Dree as she raced out of the cavern.

Dree didn't even stop to look at him. There was no time.

Her family was in that school, and if it was burning, they were all in danger. She needed to save them.

A memory flashed by: a little girl in the moonlight making a promise she couldn't keep.

"You're not," she snapped. "You've done enough."

"I can help—"

"I don't want your help!"

Lourdvang crouched onto the ledge ahead of her, extending a hind leg so she could scramble up onto his back. She was just about to jump on when Marcus grabbed her arm and pulled her to a stop. She relented, turning back to him for just a moment.

"Please," he said.

"Let go of me—"

"I need to help," he said sharply. "Don't you understand?"

She paused for just a moment, feeling sudden warmth where his slender hand was locked on her arm. She recognized the burning sensation. Fire—just waiting to erupt.

Dree knew she couldn't leave him there anyway. Some of the more aggressive dragons might decide they no longer wanted a human hanging around their lair, in which case they might kill him when Erdath wasn't around. Leaving him alone could be sentencing him to death. More importantly, whatever else Marcus represented, she still had a strong feeling she would need him to defeat the drones. He certainly understood them better than she did.

"Get on," she barked.

Marcus nodded and climbed on after her, once again

wrapping his arms around her waist. She quickly dug her fingers into the scales on Lourdvang's neck and nodded.

"Let's move!"

Lourdvang didn't waste any time. He launched himself into the air and beat his wings more frantically than she had ever seen before, propelling them through the sky like a cannonball. He gained altitude very fast and then half flew, half dove back toward the city, moving so quickly that Dree could barely open her eyes against the screaming wind.

As they flew, images of her family in the school raced through Dree's mind. She thought back to when Abi was seven, walking with Dree through the south end of the docks. It was already evening—Dree had picked Abi up from rehearsal for a play at school and walked her back, as she had just started at Master Wilhelm's and was working until evening herself. They had to pass a seedy tavern on the way, perched at the edge of the docks. It was a rickety old structure of rotting beams, filled with drunks lurching through the darkness, slurring and vomiting on the street. Dree and Abi stayed on the far side of the road, but as they passed a dark alley, a hand suddenly reached out and grabbed Abi's shoulder.

"Ain't you a pretty thing," the foul man slurred, stepping out of the shadows.

Dree reacted instantly. She turned around and punched the grizzled older man right in the mouth, dropping him in a splatter of hot blood. As soon as he hit the cobblestone she kicked him hard in the arm, hearing a snap as she broke a bone.

Dree looked down at him in disgust. "Touch her again and I'll kill you," she spat.

She left him there, a groaning pile of rags. As they quickly walked away from the scene, Abi looked up at her big sister, her eyes betraying a mixture of surprise and fear.

"What was that about?" she asked.

Dree stopped and looked at her. "There are a lot of bad people out there," she said, taking Abi's hand in hers. "Trust me. But I promise, I will never let anything happen to you. If that means knocking out a few wretched drunks, all the better." She grinned. "Remind me to teach you how to punch."

Abi laughed and hugged her tightly, and Dree remembered being afraid even then that she couldn't keep her promise forever. As much as she tried to shield her sister, there was just so much darkness and evil in the world. Now, just two years later, she had already failed her.

It wasn't long before Dree saw black smoke on the horizon, spewing out of the wrecks that now littered the south end of the city. It seemed the drones were mostly attacking the poorer outskirts. That part of the city was a war zone.

"Faster!" she shouted, fighting off an image of her little sister in the flames. If anything happened to Abi, she didn't know what she would do.

Lourdvang tightened his body into an arrow point and dove toward the ground, faster than he'd ever gone before. Dree and Marcus leaned forward as well, lest they risk being blown right off his back by the raging wind. Dree spotted the school near the shore and saw flames shooting out from the roof like flickering candles. Fire raged all across the area. There were no soldiers to be seen—obviously they had fallen back to the palace.

Above the neighborhood, drones raced across the sky, leveling everything. They made one undiscerning pass after another, destroying homes and shops and carts with equal ferocity. And in the middle of it all, the school was burning, already half-destroyed.

"What should we do?" Lourdvang growled over the wind.

"Drop us and get out of there!" Dree said, preparing to jump off as soon as they touched the ground. She felt her skin burning, but she didn't care. She had to save them.

"I won't leave you—" Lourdvang objected.

"Lead the drones away," she shouted. "Buy us some time."

Lourdvang seemed to think about that. "Be careful," he said.

Dree glanced back at Marcus, who was watching the scene in horror. His hands were trembling on Dree's waist, but he had to leave them there or risk flying off of Lourdvang's back. He wondered if she thought he was a coward—if she did, she was probably right. Either way, he was going to help her.

"Are you ready?" she asked.

Marcus nodded, trying to act brave. "Let's do it."

Dree turned back and tightened her grip, her eyes on the raging battle.

"Take us in!"

Chapter 15

Lourdvang swept onto the chewed-up road in front of the
school, landing right amid the smoking ruins. Marcus
and Dree leapt off his back and darted for the school, and
in a moment Lourdvang was gone again, spraying fire at a
passing drone and then climbing rapidly toward the skies,
hoping to draw them away. Dree watched him go, concerned.

They stopped in front of the main entrance, which was
completely engulfed in flames. They looked at each other,
uncertain of what to do.

"I'm going for it," Dree said firmly. "The fire doesn't
hurt me."

She didn't know that for sure, of course—she'd never
been completely immersed in flames. Neither had Marcus,

but he wasn't about to stand there and watch. The drones were momentarily distracted by Lourdvang, but that wouldn't last long. Marcus saw two of them hovering over the city even now, silently watching the events.

At any moment they could unleash missiles and turn the school into a crater.

"Me either," he said, wincing as the fire crackled.

"Suit yourself," Dree muttered, and then ran straight into the flames, grabbing the steel door handle with her bare hands. As she had thought, it was warm—hot, actually—but it didn't burn her skin. Whatever magic was in her blood, it blocked her from the fire.

Marcus chased after her, expecting to roast like a ham. But he too made it through the fire unscathed, and he looked around in utter disbelief as the flames rolled over him but didn't burn. Sweat dripped down his face almost instantly, but that was all.

What am I? he wondered.

Dree threw the door open and they raced inside, where the main hallway was thick with smoke. Fire was raging everywhere, shooting out of classroom doorways and racing along the ceiling. It was like the fire was alive, enjoying its deadly work.

Dree froze. She had seen this before. She remembered a hallway wrapped in fire, pictures of people she knew melting on the walls. There was smoke everywhere, but she could see. She could see past the wall of fire, where another door was waiting . . . closed.

"Gavri," she whispered. "I'm sorry."

Marcus watched as her eyes glazed over, and he heard the quiet name on her lips. He grabbed her arm and shook her. "Dree? Are you all right?"

Dree snapped back to reality and remembered that this was a different fire.

"Yes," she said. "Let's go."

The blaze seemed less frenzied farther down the hall, and that was where Dree led them, ducking low beneath the heavy smoke that hung over them like brooding clouds.

They may have been safe from the flames, but she knew the smoke could still kill them both if they didn't move quickly. Dree guessed the families would be sheltered in the mess hall—it was a huge, reinforced concrete room and would be the best option to escape the barrage. Dree had gone to this school as a child, but she left to get her job at the forge. She had bad memories of this place—fellow students calling her dragon lover and traitor and saying her dad was a cripple.

She remembered returning home one day, finding her father alone.

"What's wrong, princess?" he asked, perched in his chair.

He'd been injured only a few months earlier, but the exhaustion was already settling into his face. People still came by—revolutionaries from the underground searching for their leader—but they found only a suddenly old man in a chair. They left disappointed.

"Nothing," Dree murmured, trying to hurry to her room.

"Dree," he said sternly.

She stopped, wringing her hands together.

"The kids at school."

"What did they do?" he asked.

She looked up at him. "They called you a cripple. The older boys. They said you got what you deserved."

Her father was silent for a moment. "Come here."

Dree shuffled into his arms, and he met her eyes.

"People will always say things, princess. It doesn't matter. All that matters are our choices, Dree. Not about what you feel or fear. About what you believe."

Dree's eyes watered. "So get up. Help the people at the door—"

"Maybe one day," he said softly. "For now, I have to rest."

And just like that he was gone again, and Dree was back in the fire, racing down the hallway to save her family.

Marcus stayed right on her tail, terrified and exhilarated all at once that he could be in here, surrounded by flames. He did feel the smoke hitting him hard, though, and he suspected he'd succumb to it soon enough. A wooden door collapsed next to him, spewing fire as it did. He saw hand-drawn pictures on the wall, burning. Ahead, Dree looked manic.

"Hurry!" she shouted, sprinting down the hall.

They reached the mess hall and Dree wrenched the double doors open, revealing at least a hundred terrified people huddling in the center of the huge room. She spotted her parents with Abi and the boys and ran over to them, wrapping Abi in a fierce hug. Her father overlapped them both, tears of relief streaming down his face. Dree had never seen him cry before.

"We thought you were gone," he whispered.

"I thought the same about you," Dree replied hoarsely, pulling away from them. "What are you still doing in here? The school is on fire."

"What can we do?" he said, looking around. "It hasn't spread in here yet, and the machines are still attacking out there. We could hear the screams. If we leave we might be gunned down."

"If you stay you'll burn," Dree replied. "It's spreading fast."

"Who's that?" Abi asked, looking at Marcus.

They all turned to Marcus, who was standing awkwardly behind Dree, trying not to intrude on the tearful reunion. He managed a wan smile and a wave.

"A friend," Dree said shortly, as her mom wrapped her in a hug as well. Her eyes were puffy and red from crying, and as she stroked Dree's cheek, the tears started again.

"We thought—"

"I know," Dree cut in. "But we can do this later. We have to leave."

"How?" Abi asked, terrified.

Marcus looked back and saw that the fire was now raging across the doorway they had entered. He spotted another door on the far side of the mess hall and hurried over to check it. Gingerly pulling it open, he saw that the fire was already spreading there too, but that it was not nearly as fierce as the other side. It was the only way out of the gym.

"Here!" he called. "Hurry!"

Dree and her family started herding everyone toward

the door, and Marcus cringed when he saw all the small children huddled against their parents. There were even babies cradled in their mothers' arms. He couldn't let anything happen to these people.

Marcus quickly led the crowd out into the hallway, where the flames were already creeping along the walls and floors like vines. Screams suddenly erupted from the mess hall, and he looked back to see that the far wall had just collapsed beneath the fire.

They didn't have much time.

Waving his hand and shouting for the crowd to follow, he turned left down the hallway, heading for what looked like daylight some fifty feet away. Dree was still at the back of the group, trying to get everyone out, so it was up to Marcus to lead the way.

He was halfway there when the school was rocked by a powerful explosion. The force of it almost knocked him right off his feet, as up ahead another wall collapsed.

"Hurry!" he shouted, and the crowd of screaming Draconians broke into a run.

One harried young woman pulling a child beside her was just passing Marcus when the ceiling started to give out. A wooden beam fell right through, bursting with flames and heading straight for the woman and her child. Marcus didn't even think.

He reached up and caught the beam, almost buckling under the weight but just managing to keep his footing. The fire was racing over his hands, but as before, it didn't burn him. The weight was incredible though, and he felt his arms straining terribly.

"Go!" he screamed.

The woman stared at him, wide-eyed, and then ran out with her boy. The rest of the group rushed past, gasping when they saw Marcus holding the burning beam over his head, the fire seemingly having no effect on him. Dree and her family came last, and she helped him push the beam aside, looking at him with a strange expression.

There was no time to talk. The school was rocked by another explosion, and Marcus and Dree ran down the hallway as the ceiling started to cave in. Her family burst out of the back door, and Dree and Marcus followed, racing into the brilliant daylight as the hallway collapsed behind them. Their hearts sank immediately. The crowd was huddled together in a circle, right in the middle of a field outside the school. There, hovering right in front of them, were three drones.

The drones weren't firing—they just floated there, red eyes locked on the crowd. Machine gun turrets were exposed below each of their wings. The silence was heavy.

"What are they waiting for?" Dree whispered.

"I don't know," Marcus said. "Orders, maybe."

A man suddenly broke away from the crowd, sprinting for cover. He never made it—one drone casually gunned him down, not even moving from its position. The screams and weeping echoed across the field.

Marcus felt sick. Were resources really worth all this?

He stepped forward, walking toward the drones.

"Hey!" he said. "My name is Marcus Brimley from

Arlington, Virginia. Please stand down. These people are not your enemies!"

He stopped in front of the drones, pleading.

"Please...stop these attacks. You're murdering children—"

The drones suddenly shot upward, about fifty feet overhead. For just a moment, Marcus thought that he had persuaded them to stop. Then he saw a white drone waiting beneath the clouds, almost invisible, missiles emerging from its stark wings. The red eyes of the black drones flared as they locked on their target: the crowd.

"Take cover!" Marcus screamed, already knowing they would never make it.

But just as the drones prepared to fire, black shapes swooped from the sky. Marcus looked up in wonder as the dragons descended like a flock of ravens, spewing fire and converging on the three drones.

Erdath landed directly on top of one of the black drones, tearing at the heavy metal with his teeth and claws in an absolutely terrifying fervor. He ripped a wing clean off with his teeth, sending sparks shooting everywhere. Erdath released it, letting it smash into the ground, a ruined hulk.

The dragons turned after the two remaining drones, but the drones didn't fight back. They simply took off to the south, leaving the attacking dragons far behind them.

Marcus and Dree watched as the drones vanished into the distance. Lourdvang and Erdath landed in front of the crowd.

"Thank you," Dree said, hurrying forward to hug Lourdvang.

DRAGONS VS. DRONES

The other Draconians looked afraid, but many echoed her sentiment.

Erdath looked around the crowd. "You should leave the city. Make for the mountains. There are old dragon caves there—bring food and water and go."

The crowd quickly dispersed, many of them stopping to thank Marcus and Dree before they took off into the burning streets. The young mother Marcus had saved stopped in front of him, her young son huddled against her leg.

"Thank you," she said hoarsely. "Are you all right?"

Marcus blushed. "Yeah. I'm fine."

She glanced at her son, then back to Marcus and lowered her voice. "How did you do that?"

"Luck," Marcus said, shifting awkwardly and feeling Erdath's curious eyes on him. "Take your son and get to the mountains. It will be safer there."

She nodded. "Thank you."

She took off with her son, and Marcus turned back to Dree, who was giving her family instructions on how to get to Lourdvang's hidden cave in the nearby mountain. They looked scared but determined, especially Abi. Dree took her father's arm.

"We'll fly overhead to keep the skies clear," she said. "Get some supplies and go right away. It will take you an hour or two to get there. Don't go back to the docks."

"Maybe we should try the bunkers?" Dree's mother suggested.

Dree shook her head. "They won't protect you. Get to the mountains."

She hugged her family and then hopped onto Lourdvang's back. The other dragons were circling ahead, black shapes against the sky. There were at least fifty dragons there, and Dree knew the rest of the city was probably in a panic. Marcus followed Dree onto Lourdvang's back and watched as her family hurried into the city.

Lourdvang leapt into the air, and Marcus took a last look behind them, where the school was now a flaming heap of metal and concrete. If he didn't think of something soon, there would be nothing left of Dracone to save. He wondered again who was controlling the drones. Could it really be the U.S. government? Would they really murder all these people just for resources?

As they circled over the city, he spotted a black speck flitting over the tilled farm fields to the south. It must have been one of the smaller drones that Ralar had described, not much bigger than Lightning Bug. It looked like it was surveying the landscape. The drone flew in a carefully organized grid, moving slowly as it swept over one acre at a time, just like Bug in a storm. In fact, they looked almost identical.

Marcus turned away, adjusting his grip on Dree's waist and watching as her family hurried to grab their supplies, as small as ants below. The city was crumbling around them, the entire block nothing but rubble.

Whoever it was controlling the drones, they were winning.

Chapter 16

Marcus, Dree, and Lourdvang stood together on the exposed ledge outside the Nightwings' lair, staring at the lush green valley far below them. Multicolored birds were circling over the forest canopy, their shrill voices echoing through the mountains.

Marcus, Dree, and Lourdvang had circled overhead for hours while Dree's family made the ascent to the cave. It wasn't an easy climb, but unfortunately without fire-resistant armor, none of them could climb onto Lourdvang. Only when Dree's family was safely tucked into the cave did Dree, Marcus, and Lourdvang return to the den. They needed a plan.

Dree's mind was on her father. He had looked ashamed

as he stood before Lourdvang and Erdath—afraid to meet their eyes and stealing furtive, bewildered looks, as if he was staring into the past and wondering if he could still return to it. At one point she had seen him wipe his eyes gruffly with his sleeve. She knew he was probably thinking of his dragon, Delpath. Delpath had been killed many years before by hunters, a few years after the split between humans and dragons, and she knew her father still mourned him every day. He refused to even look at the merchant stands in the city. When she thought of Lourdvang being killed for his fangs and scales and heart, she wondered how he could even look at humans without hatred.

Marcus's thoughts were elsewhere. The flight back to the mountains had been a silent one as he stared out at the devastated landscape. The drones had laid waste to some of the outlying towns as well, leaving hollowed-out ruins and bodies in the soil. Once or twice he thought he saw an almost ghostly black dot slip in and out of the clouds on the horizon. They were watching, waiting, and Marcus still suspected that the attacks would not end until Dracone was devoid of all sentient life. If he was right, the U.S. government could then waltz in through the portal, push the smoking ruins aside, and strip the world bare.

The idea made him feel sick and ashamed. He wondered again if his father had known about all this. If that was why George Brimley had traveled to Dracone, and why he had never come back. Maybe he was just trying to save this beautiful world from his own people. Marcus wanted to believe it so badly that it already seemed true. His father was no traitor. He was a hero that had been betrayed by his own government.

That hope was the only thing keeping Marcus going. His father was somewhere in Dracone, and Marcus was going to find him and help him shut that portal forever. But first he had to stop the drones.

When they returned to the den, Marcus sought out Erdath to ask why he had decided to help. The ancient dragon had taken a long time to answer.

"Because a decade of hate does not erase a thousand years of friendship," he said at last, smoke curling out of his nostrils as if he was puffing on a cigar. "If we do not work together, we will both be destroyed."

Work together, Marcus thought to himself.

"So what now?" Dree asked, her eyes on the flitting red and yellow birds.

Marcus shook his head. "I don't know. I thought maybe I could reprogram one of the drones, but how am I supposed to get one to stand still long enough to hook up my laptop? The only one that isn't flying around shooting things is lying in the middle of—"

Marcus stopped. He slowly turned to Dree, his mind racing.

"You're a welder."

Dree was already way ahead of him. "I wouldn't know how to rebuild—"

"You wouldn't have to make it the exact same as it was,"

Marcus cut in, running through the necessary logistics. The main computer processor would still be there. The propulsion engines. The weapons. "You could design it how you want."

He grinned, turning to Lourdvang and eyeing his massive wings and scales.

"In fact, we could probably make some improvements."

Dree frowned, following his gaze. "What are you talking about?"

"What if we combined the technology of the drones with the maneuverability and intelligence and fire of a dragon? A hybrid of the two. It would be far more powerful than the existing drones—it could wipe them out."

Dree was skeptical. The toy dragonfly was one thing, but building something the size of Lourdvang sounded nearly impossible. Everything would have to be on a larger scale. Still, if she had the drone structure to build upon, it might be feasible. It was ambitious, but maybe not impossible. Besides, she didn't exactly have a better plan.

"We would need more materials," she said. "And torches."

"Can we steal that from Wilhelm's?"

Dree considered that. "Maybe, but I think we'd need more than he has in stock." She suddenly thought of something. "The steel mill where my mom works—they have tons of raw metal and welding equipment. She told me it's abandoned now—the drones hit it soon after she left. We could get everything we need there."

Marcus turned to Lourdvang. "We're going to need—"

"Dragons," Lourdvang said. "I'll get two of them to

take you to the drone. They can lift it back here together. Dree and I will go to the mill to get the materials we need."

Marcus grinned. "Perfect."

"You're serious about this?" Dree asked.

"Very," Marcus said, the grin slipping off his face. "In fact, it may be our only chance to save Dracone."

⊕

Lourdvang and Dree landed outside the steel mill, both of them solemn. The massive factory was abandoned, a smoking hole puncturing the side and revealing tangled clumps of machinery within. It had been built almost a decade earlier, at the beginning of the economic revolution, and it had been churning out steel products ever since.

Dree slipped off of Lourdvang's back and checked the evening sky, feeling her skin prickle. The city was eerily silent, which only made her more anxious. She almost wished she could see a drone. Not knowing where they were was even more terrifying. She felt like one was going to pop out at any moment and blow them to pieces.

"Move quickly," Lourdvang grumbled, obviously thinking the same thing.

She darted over to the storage yard and combed through the stacks of processed metal. There were huge steel girders and frames and cart axles, as well as long sheets and tin roof slats. She laid the most ideal pieces into a pile, making sure they were arranged so Lourdvang could easily scoop them up in his claws. She selected thin sheet metal, pipes and pistons, and steel girders, as well as smaller scrap materials that could be crafted into the more detailed sections and inner mechanisms. She didn't understand the drones, but she understood steel and movement and flight. She would have to build the dragonfly toy on a massive scale—capable of intricate in-flight maneuvers and yet sturdy enough to withstand missiles and machine gun fire. Marcus told her there wasn't even anything like it in his world, and they were far ahead of Dracone in terms of technology.

But Marcus pointed out that his world also didn't have magic, and the dragons exuded it. With Lourdvang's help, he was confident they could make it work. Marcus was a different person when he had a mission: He was focused and passionate and optimistic.

He was pretty much the only one. Erdath and the other dragons had immediately dismissed the idea and thought that the mere notion of a dragon/drone hybrid was unseemly. But Marcus had at least persuaded them to help gather the scraps.

When she had collected enough materials, Dree sprinted into the mill to find the welding equipment. The inside was still thick with dust and lingering smoke, blurring a scene of an obviously panicked escape. Scattered clothes and boots and tools lay everywhere, dropped onto the concrete and forgotten. Gloomy sunlight was pouring in through the massive hole in the wall, but otherwise the building was dark. It took her a while to track the equipment down, but finally she managed to find torches, spare tanks, and a few other small items that would allow her to craft the finer joints and gears: casts and scrap iron that she could use Lourdvang's fire to forge.

She passed a door in the dreary darkness and paused, thinking that it seemed out of place. There was a large DO NOT ENTER sign affixed to the heavy stainless steel, but it was hardly necessary. A massive padlock sat above the handle, and another bolt ran along the top. Nobody was getting in there without a key, though she didn't see a slot.

Dree was just heading back outside when she noticed a huge shadow darkening the doorway. Lourdvang was huddled against the wall, clearly hiding from something. She gingerly stepped outside, following his gaze upward. There was a solitary drone far overhead, moving slowly and silently across the sky. She could see the fiery red eye scanning the ground below, and she wondered what it was looking for. What was it doing? Why not fire on the city now and finish its work? Why wait and watch in silence? It didn't make any sense.

"I saw it a few minutes ago," Lourdvang said. "We'll wait until it passes."

They waited there, huddled against the cool steel wall and watching the drone fade into the distance. Dree clutched the heavy welding equipment against her stomach.

When the sky was clear, they hurried into the storage yard. Lourdvang scooped up the big pile of metal in his front claws while Dree lugged the bulky welding equipment up onto his back.

"Try and take it slow," she said, setting everything on her lap.

"No problem," he rumbled. "Other than the murderous drones patrolling the city."

"Was that sarcasm?" she asked, raising an eyebrow.

"I'm learning."

Dree snorted as Lourdvang flapped his wings and lifted slowly off the ground, skipping his usual bounding leap. She tried to hold on to the equipment and still keep a hand on his scales, but she eventually gave up. She'd just have to hope he didn't make any sudden turns, or she would go flying off his back with the equipment.

Dree watched the horizon carefully as they flew out of the city, but other than a fleeting glimpse of black to the south, she saw nothing except exodus and mounting defense. The poorer people in the scattered towns and villages were heading downtown in great masses, seeking shelter in the so-far untouched shops and buildings of the downtown core. The ivory palace also remained intact, tall and gleaming in the middle of the destruction. But how long would that last? As far as Dree was concerned, they were all just sheep going to the slaughter.

The sun was just starting to set over the mountains, casting a brilliant orange glow over the sky. They flew toward it slowly, Lourdvang obviously beset by the heavy weight. He was forced to flap his massive wings almost constantly to stay aloft.

They were almost to the den when Dree saw the strangest sight of her life. In the distance, it looked like a great, lumbering dragon was barely making it across the sky, holding some sort of enormous prey in its talons. As they closed in, she realized it was two black dragons carrying the demolished drone between them, Marcus looking on in concern from the back of one. He was leaning over to keep an eye on the drone.

"Careful!" he shouted over the wind.

Dree couldn't help but smile. Marcus was so intent on his project that he was yelling at a dragon, which was never a good idea. Perhaps there was a lot more to the gangly boy than met the eye.

They all set down on the overhanging ledge at the same time, the drone clanging loudly off the stone just as Lourdvang released the huge pile of metal. Dree and Marcus leapt off their respective dragons, and Marcus hurried over to her, grinning as he looked at the materials. He was already running through a mental checklist.

"Perfect," he said. "Did you see that drone over the city?"

Dree nodded. "What do you think it was doing?"

"Surveying the next attack. Which means we have to move quickly."

He turned toward the cavern, but Dree grabbed his arm.

"Do you really think this will work?"

Marcus paused. "I have no idea. But we have to try." He walked over to one of the two dragons that had retrieved the drone. "Can we get this inside?" he asked, inspecting the haul.

The dragon growled at him, black smoke spewing like

a fog and completely covering Marcus. Marcus slowly reappeared as the murky cloud dissipated. He didn't say anything for a moment, and then he walked over to the pile of metal and started grabbing pieces. Lourdvang roared with laughter and then started to help.

Dree just sighed. This was going to be interesting.

She hurried into the cavern to prepare her tools. It was time to get to work.

Chapter 17

The work was incredibly grueling. Night came and went by the light of a welding torch as Dree and Marcus disassembled the ruined drone, harvesting its processing core and other essential components and putting the hull aside to be rebuilt into their hybrid dragon. They were set up in a small side cavern where they would have some privacy, but curious dragons popped in constantly to watch. On the plus side, it kept the cavern warm.

Dree was astounded by the seemingly infinite pieces within the drone. Her creations were much simpler, but Marcus said the mechanisms could still be combined with the electronics and power cells of the drone technology. With his programming knowledge, her welding skills, and Lourdvang's inherent understanding of dragon flight, they had a slim chance of making something that could actually fight the drones.

Dree was unconvinced, but she was certainly going to try. It weighed on her constantly that her family was huddled in a cave, safe but stuck in the darkness, far from home. And even there, the drones would find them eventually. Nowhere was completely safe.

As they worked, Marcus outlined what they knew about the drones.

"There are three types," he said as he carefully removed some of the inner mechanisms. "The red-eyed ones—Trackers. We know they keep a watch on the city, maybe looking for targets. They have dual machine guns and light missiles."

"I know," Dree said dryly. "I'm looking at one as we speak."

Marcus ignored her. "Then we have the white ones—we'll call them Destroyers. They seem to swoop in for the major attacks. Probably heavy armor, definitely heavy-duty machine guns and missiles." He removed a delicate wire and placed it in the pile. "And finally we have the little ones—Researchers. I think they're just collecting data and surveying the countryside. Maybe for resources. I doubt they're armed, but it would be light weaponry if they are."

Dree thought about that as she removed an armored plate.

"So they have three types, and we have a hybrid that probably won't even work."

Marcus sighed. "Yep."

After they had disassembled the drone, aided at times by

Lourdvang's fearsome claws, Marcus took the processing core and sat in the corner with his laptop. He managed to extract the main processor chip from the drone's core and plug it into his computer. An endless stream of code popped up on his screen, and he took a breath. This was not going to be easy.

But he had the picture of the coding on the wall, and he suspected the clue to all of this was hidden somewhere in there. It would just take hours—or days—to decipher. While he worked on that, Dree began the most complex welding job of her life. She had no schematics or designs. She was working solely on instinct, along with the gentle advice of Lourdvang, who watched over everything. He had never seen her weld before, but he had an innate fascination for building. It wasn't a dragon trait.

Late into the night they took a break to sleep, and Dree and Marcus lay down on the hard stone next to Lourdvang—both using their packs as pillows. It was cold up in the mountains, but with Lourdvang there, it was like sleeping next to a burning hearth. Marcus fidgeted on the ground, staring up at the shadows. Everything was pitch-black.

"Your family seemed nice," he said. "You look like your dad."

"People tell me that sometimes," Dree said. "Do you miss your family?"

Marcus paused. "I don't really have one. My dad's best friend has been taking care of me since he left, but my mom died when I was very young. I never knew her."

Dree glanced over at his shadowy form. They were

close—only a few feet apart—but she could barely make him out. "How long has your father been missing?"

"Eight years," he said quietly.

"And you have been searching all this time?"

"I'll search the rest of my life, if I have to."

"How do you know he's alive?"

"I just know." Marcus looked at her. "Can I ask you something?"

"Sure."

"You said the name Gavri earlier, in the school. Who is that?"

Dree was silent for a long time. She didn't talk about Gavri with anyone—not even Abi. But for some reason it was easier to talk to Marcus. She felt comfortable with him, like she somehow knew he would understand her pain and guilt better than most. "My little brother. He's dead."

"I'm sorry," Marcus said. "When?"

"About seven years ago. I was five."

"What happened?"

Lourdvang shifted beside Dree, obviously wondering if she would confide in Marcus. Lourdvang knew the story—all of it. He knew how much it tormented her.

"He died in a fire," she said finally. "My house burned down."

Marcus glanced at her. "That's terrible. I'm sorry."

Dree didn't know why she said the next thing. It just came out.

"I started it."

It tore Dree apart to admit it, and she immediately wondered what Marcus would think of her. That she was a murderer. A freak. Maybe he would leave.

Marcus just lay there for a moment, unsure of how to reply. "Why?"

"I didn't mean to," she whispered, her voice cracking just a little. "I was angry. My parents sent me to my room. I felt this . . . heat, and I couldn't stop it. I let it pour out onto my bed, and the fire started spreading everywhere. It moved so quickly. I didn't know what to do—I just froze and watched it. When I finally realized what was happening, I ran to get my family. My dad dragged me out, but Gavri . . . he didn't make it. They had to leave him behind."

Tears streamed down her cheeks, but she didn't wipe them. In the darkness she could finally cry again. She could let it out—the memories that followed her everywhere.

"That's not your fault," Marcus said.

"It is," she replied numbly. "I started it. And I could have saved him. The fire didn't hurt me. But my dad dragged me out." She turned away. "I can still hear him screaming."

Marcus reached out in the darkness and found her hand.

"You were five," he said gently. "You didn't have a choice."

Dree let him hold her hand—she let the warmth flow through her.

"Maybe," she said at last. "But that doesn't stop the memories."

Marcus squeezed her fingers. "Those won't stop until you let them."

They let those words hang in the air until both succumbed to the darkness.

⊕

The days passed in a haze. Dragon sentries returned once in a while with reports of attacks, but soon those too blurred together. Houses destroyed, buildings leveled, fields of dead Outliers shot from the sky and left to dissolve into the soil. The Sages were long gone, the Nightwings were hidden in Forost, and the Flames were secluded in the Teeth, so the Outliers and the humans were taking the brunt of the drone's attacks.

The stories were of death, and it only made them work faster.

They didn't speak of the fire again, but Marcus and Dree both felt that a wall had disappeared between them. They were comfortable in their silence. Dree was relieved that Marcus knew the truth about her and still hadn't left, and he was relieved that she trusted him enough to share her secrets. He hoped it meant she had forgiven him for leading the drones into Dracone.

Dree may have felt some relief from her guilt, but Marcus's was growing worse. With every story from the sentries, his stomach hardened into stone. They had to hurry.

A week passed, and a rudimentary hybrid began to take shape. With Lourdvang's help, Dree built wings from the sheet metal—designed more for maneuverability and speed than lift. The drones had the engines; she just needed to improve on the design. Crude legs and claws were formed and attached to the central frame of the drone, built on pistons and cogs. The wiring of the drone was completely intact, and Marcus showed Dree how to run it through the hybrid. But technology was not enough. In places she showed him where fire could power movement, and Lourdvang proved very useful in that matter, pointing out things that made no sense to Marcus. And yet when they created the shape, Lourdvang blew fire in the heart and limbs began to move. For Marcus it was hard to fathom, but he realized it was their only chance.

Somehow the fire had the ability to power things in a way that didn't make sense on Earth—fire didn't move objects by itself. It needed a whole internal combustion system or water to turn to steam. Obviously this was not regular fire as Marcus understood it. When he asked Dree about it, she just shrugged and said dragon fire had always been considered magical among the dragon riders of old. Marcus wanted to study it more, but they didn't have the time. So he just watched in fascination as the combination of Lourdvang's fire and the drone's circuitry and engines brought the hybrid to life.

Even fire couldn't bring artificial intelligence and voice command though, so Marcus spent most of his time restructuring the code. He used the one written on the wall as a guide and found that it did outline how to create open-ended code. They were instructions, and he could use them to give the hybrid limited intelligence. It was essential: A robot that responded to commands wouldn't be enough. They needed a weapon that understood how to fight.

Twelve days after they started, the hybrid was ready for its first test. The time had passed quickly, despite the arduous work. Stories of destruction in the city and the outskirts had continued to pour in from dragon scouts, and Dree worried constantly about her family. She and Lourdvang hadn't dared risk a visit to the hidden cave, however, for fear of attracting unwanted attention. Marcus and Dree had also slept very little, and both were wavering as they stood in the shadowy cavern, examining their creation. It was crude and unpolished, but it was still pretty impressive.

The wings were sheet metal attached to great frames of steel, bordering a rudimentary dragon shape built around the hulk of the drone. The body had been easy to fashion, but building enormous legs and a neck and even a fully formed dragon head had been feats that had driven Dree to the very edge of her patience and talent. She was fairly confident that she was the only person in Dracone who could have created something like this, and still she was skeptical. Erdath and a few other dragons were gathered at the entrance, having heard that the first test would take place that afternoon. They were even more dubious than she was, and Erdath had blown out an unhappy puff of smoke when he saw the bizarre creation.

"Well," Marcus said. "Should we try it?"

Dree glanced at him. "Might as well."

An equally tired Lourdvang lumbered over to the hybrid and leaned down to where Dree had created a large shaft to the heart of the dragon, the same as she had for the toy dragonfly. She was using the same mechanics, but with the help of powerful fuel cells and advanced wiring from the drone, which she hoped wouldn't immediately incinerate under Lourdvang's fire. Theoretically, the combination of the two power sources would allow for greater energy, more power, and a mechanical creation that bordered somewhere in a dangerous place between technology and magic.

"Do it," Dree said, chewing on a nail nervously.

Lourdvang nodded and sprayed fire into the shaft, trying to keep the blaze narrow and focused. It shot into the hybrid, which instantly lit it up like a candle, an orange glow beaming out from every opening. Marcus fidgeted anxiously, focused on the eyes. The processing core was placed in the heart of the hybrid, right where it had been originally, but they had worked hard to run wires up to the head as well. Nothing happened.

The hybrid lit up the cavern, but it didn't move.

Dree scowled and threw her torch on the ground. "I knew it wouldn't work."

Marcus remained silent as Dree walked over to the hybrid.

"It's too big," she ranted, feeling the heat rise up in her. "And the wires and computer parts and whatever else you said—it doesn't mix with fire. We're wasting time in here when we should be figuring out a way to—"

"Baby Hybrid," Marcus said calmly. "Stand up."

He didn't know if it would work for sure, of course. But he thought he saw a flicker of light in the eyes. As soon as he spoke, they flared orange. The hybrid immediately climbed to its feet, all straining metal and groaning and noise like a factory churning to life. Dree froze and stared wide-eyed as it stood up, half as big as Lourdvang but still massive. It waited there silently, its legs firm and steady.

"Impossible," she whispered.

"Obviously not," Marcus replied, cracking a lopsided grin.

Lourdvang looked leery of the hybrid, as did Erdath and the other dragons. They also looked stunned, which was exactly how Dree and Marcus felt.

"Baby Hybrid," Marcus said. "Fly."

Instantly, the engines began to hum. They had managed to relocate the propulsion engines of the drones to the back of each stationary wing and kept the main one on the bottom to ensure that the hybrid could hover and maintain altitude. The hybrid didn't need to flap its wings, but it could angle them slightly for better maneuverability. The engines flared, receiving full power, and the hybrid began to slowly lift off the floor.

Dree shrieked with laughter as it started floating into the air. "I can't believe it," she said, grabbing Marcus by the shoulder. "It's amazing—"

The words were barely out of her mouth when the engines sputtered and went out. The hybrid fell three feet onto the hard stone floor, and one of the huge legs snapped right off at the weld. The entire thing slammed into a heap and went dark. Dree and Marcus just stood there for a moment, unable to speak.

Erdath and the other dragons chuckled and left. Lourdvang pawed the hybrid, as if testing to see if it was really defunct.

Marcus shrugged. "Let's try it again."

DRAGONS VS. DRONES

That night, Marcus and Dree sat across from each other examining the hybrid's wiring. Marcus was explaining how it worked, and Dree listened, fascinated. Even Lourdvang was curled up beside them, watching intently as Marcus explained about electric transmissions, polarization, and programming. These were things Marcus had loved since he was a kid, and he wasn't used to anyone listening so intently, never mind a girl and her dragon. He was flushing as she asked questions and shook her head in amazement.

"Does everyone know these things where you come from?" Dree asked.

Marcus smiled. "No. I was a bit . . . keen on this stuff."

"So you must have been important."

"Not quite," Marcus said awkwardly.

They had a small lantern lit beside them, which Erdath had kept stored from years earlier when humans used to frequent Forost. Dree had lit it with her finger, and Marcus had stared at her in wonder of his own as the freshly born shadows leapt over their faces.

"They don't really value these things in junior high school," Marcus added. "I didn't have a lot of friends. Never did, really."

He was exhausted, with dark circles around his eyes and bags below them. His hair was tangled and greasy, matted against his forehead with long-dried sweat, and he didn't even want to know what he smelled like.

But he knew Dree didn't care. For one thing, she was just as dirty, and maybe worse. Her face was scorched black from the welding, and her hair was a knotted mess.

"Me either," Dree admitted.

"Why not? An awesome girl like—" Marcus stopped, flushing.

Lourdvang snorted. "I think he complimented you."

"I got that," Dree said dryly. "Thank you, but I have Lourdvang and Abi. They are all I need." She paused. "And I guess I never really took the time to try. I was thinking about other things."

"The past," Marcus replied quietly. "Same with me. I just wanted to find my dad."

"And I just wanted to save my brother," Dree whispered.

They were silent for a moment.

"How about we save Dracone instead?" he offered. "And call it even."

Dree smiled. "Deal."

They sat there until the torch had burned out and then lay down next to Lourdvang to sleep. Marcus stared up into the darkness, his hands behind his head.

"That was pretty sweet today."

Dree smiled. "Yeah. By the way, what's with the name Baby Hybrid?"

"I don't know. I was just calling it that in my head all along, and so I programmed that name into the processor. What do you think?"

"It's stupid," Lourdvang rumbled.

Dree burst out laughing. "Sorry. We're still working on his social skills."

"I see that," Marcus said sourly. "Well, I can change it if you want."

"No," Dree replied. "I like it. Let's make Baby Hybrid fly."

Marcus looked over at her. "Can I ask you something?"

"Sure."

"The fire you started . . . with your hands. What is it? Have you always been able to do that?"

Dree stared up at the ceiling. "For as long as I can remember."

"It's only started recently for me," he said quietly. "I started melting things. Does anyone else have that power here?"

"Not that I know of. It's rare. There were a few riders who had it, but not many. What about in your world?"

Marcus snorted. "Definitely not. We don't have a lot of . . . magical things." He paused. "What do you think it's for? Why do we have it?"

"I don't know," Dree said. "But I'm guessing we're going to find out."

They both drifted off to sleep, but soon Dree woke with a start. She'd just been in a fire again—the house was collapsing, her family screaming. They were all there, trapped, and she couldn't get to any of them. The fire was coming fast, and she had to save them.

Leaving Marcus on the floor, she grabbed her torch and got to work.

✛

The next morning Lourdvang took Dree and Marcus to a small waterfall in the valley below Forost—a place that Dree had never seen. They had slept for an hour or two at most, and they were both absolutely filthy with sweat and grease and dirt. Dree reluctantly agreed to go with Lourdvang so that they could all wash themselves off.

As Lourdvang swept to a landing on the shore of the river, Dree was instantly glad she'd agreed. The waterfall spilled off a thirty-foot sheer cliff lined with brambles and ancient-looking oak trees that soaked up the mist. The water then crashed into a rocky pool before racing down through the valley, settling there like glass. Marcus smiled.

"It's beautiful," he said.

"Even dragons bathe once in a while," Lourdvang replied. "This is where we go. We call it the Mountains' Tears. The water is cold, but it's very fresh."

Marcus and Dree tentatively approached the water, sneaking an awkward glance at each other. It was late summer and cool in the mountains, but the sun was shining down through the peaks overhead, and it was warm enough that the water was tempting.

Dree turned and slipped off her filthy woolen shirt, leaving just a hide undershirt. Marcus immediately flushed and looked away. He had long ago taken off his fire-resistant armor, but he self-consciously stripped down to his boxer shorts and tip-toed into the water, hoping to escape notice.

He didn't really want her to see his pale, bony arms and stick legs. Lourdvang did though.

"You look like a snow rabbit," he commented, curling up by the rocks bordering the falls. "After the winter. Maybe we need to get you more food."

Marcus flushed even brighter as Dree broke out laughing. "Lourdvang! Social skills!"

Lourdvang closed his eyes. "Just an observation."

Feeling his cheeks burning, Marcus quickly waded out into the water. Goose bumps raced up his entire body. The water was freezing cold, but it was incredibly clear and the current was gentle and relaxing. Dree shot Marcus a lopsided grin and then dove into the pool like an otter, disappearing below the surface and splashing Marcus with icy water. He gasped as she emerged in the middle of the pool, heading for the waterfall.

Dree climbed up onto the rocks and proceeded to wipe the dirt and grime from her body, letting the water crash around her.

Dree looked at him. "You going to join me or what?"

Marcus hesitated and then climbed up onto the rocks beside her. They both laughed as the water pummeled them like torrential rain, and Dree had to grab Marcus's arm at one point to keep him from spilling backward into the deep water.

"Clean yet?" she called.

"I guess," he said.

"Good!"

She pushed him right off the rock, and he yelped and

plunged into the water, the current carrying him back into the gentle eddy in the middle of the pool.

After a while, they both climbed back onto the shore and dried themselves in the sun.

"Well?" Lourdvang rumbled.

"It was a good idea," Dree said.

"A very good idea," Marcus agreed, stretching out.

Marcus turned back to the sky again, looking at the snowcapped mountains and the brilliant morning sun, realizing with a start that he had barely even thought about Jack or Brian the entire time he had been in Dracone. What was wrong with him? Why did this place feel so much more right than his life in Arlington?

He tried to shake the feeling, but as he snuck a glimpse at Dree, he realized that he wasn't even sure he wanted to go home.

Beside him, Dree was thinking that she didn't want Marcus to leave either.

Two days later, the three of them gathered around the hybrid once again. If they were tired the first time they'd tested her, they were well beyond that now. They had checked over every section, and Marcus had finally realized that the power cells weren't quite aligned, which he hoped explained the outage. But Dree also had to weld the leg back on, and while she was at it, she had fortified every single joint and pivot and surface on the hybrid. She had even double plated the wings for more armor.

It was a little bulkier, but far stronger. Baby Hybrid was ready.

Without thinking, Dree reached out and took Marcus's hand. Heat raced between them, shooting tingles up both their arms, but Marcus held on. They were both nervous.

Dree nodded at Lourdvang, and he bent down in front of the shaft again.

"Here goes nothing," he growled.

He breathed a stream of fire into the hybrid, and once again, it lit up.

"Baby Hybrid," Marcus said, squeezing Dree's fingers. "Fly."

The hybrid thrummed and shifted as it stood, the engines immediately kicking in and lifting it off the ground. It was silent and smooth, just as they had hoped. It rose higher and higher, stopping about five feet from the ceiling, which was also a good sign. It meant the sensors were working and it wouldn't fly into a wall.

Marcus and Dree exchanged an anxious look.

"Follow us," Marcus said.

They hurried out into the main cavern. Baby Hybrid followed closely behind, moving slowly and shakily as it floated through the opening. The other dragons looked at them in shock as they hurried outside to the ledge, the hybrid still hovering along behind them. Its eyes blazed orange, and its metal jaw caught the morning light. It looked like some nightmarish version of a dragon, but smaller and more awkward. It was flying, though, and there were machine guns beneath each wing, as well as ten missiles sitting in the bay in its gut, left in place from the original drone.

It had all the firepower of the drones, along with the fire of a dragon.

As they walked out on the ledge, Dree and Marcus turned to the hybrid.

Marcus smiled. "Initiate flight test."

Baby Hybrid took off, still moving a bit unsteadily through the air. The engines under each wing hadn't been designed to be apart, and it was clearly trying to balance itself. But the neck straightened like it was supposed to, the legs tucked themselves in, and Baby Hybrid took off into the open sky.

Dree felt her eyes water unexpectedly. It was as if they had just created life.

The hybrid soared around for a little while, its wings shifting ever so slightly to gain height or send it into sharp turns and spirals. Marcus had programmed the drone to test itself on its first flight, and it was clearly doing that. It wasn't perfect, but it was functional.

"How do we get it to come back?" Dree asked suddenly.

Marcus grinned. "It has limited intelligence. It knows who we are and will find us when the testing is done. The drones had infrared and sensors, so it can see. Instead of taking commands remotely, it will always return to us for new instructions."

"Brilliant," Dree said.

Marcus beamed. "Thank you."

As they watched the hybrid soar around, they heard something approach from behind them. The three of them turned to find Erdath scowling.

"It works," he said, smoke billowing out of his mouth. "Sort of."

"What do you mean?" Dree asked, a little offended.

Erdath stared at the hybrid, watching it stream across the sky. "It flies, but not well. It looks like a dragon, but it is not. You have done a decent job, I admit. But you have not done enough."

Marcus slumped. "I thought it was pretty good—"

"Tell me, boy, do you think that will destroy the drones?"

Marcus turned and looked up at the hybrid. "I . . . I don't know," he admitted.

Baby Hybrid was impressive, and the fact that it was flying was almost beyond hope. But it was still a bit clunky, a bit slow, and its weaponry was a match for one of the Trackers and nothing more. Against a group of drones, it didn't have a chance.

"No, it won't," Erdath said. "While you two have been building this . . . thing, the world has been burning. Yesterday the drones killed thirty Outliers. Four drones against thirty dragons, and it was a slaughter. The countryside is aflame, and the people in your city huddle together in the downtown area, forgotten for the moment. Now the dragons are the targets."

"What are you saying?" Dree asked.

"I want your hybrid to work," Erdath said. "But this thing you have created will not destroy them. I have seen them fight—the one I killed was from luck alone. To beat them, you need something greater. You need the Egg."

Lourdvang started. "We can't—"

"You must," Erdath said. "With it you might just give that thing real dragon magic. You give it a chance."

"The dragon relic?" Marcus asked, confused. "How would that help?"

"It *may* help," Lourdvang explained, eyeing Erdath. "It is said to give great power and to be the source of a dragon's fire. Some call it the heart of the dragons. It can endow any dragon—or perhaps any*thing*—with the power of our forebears. For the hybrid, that may mean true fire . . . something like life."

Marcus watched the hybrid slowly turn around and zoom in the other direction. "Where is it?"

"That's the problem," Lourdvang said quietly.

Erdath nodded. "It is the source of all dragon power, so of course there is only one place in Dracone it could be. You must go to the Teeth. It is with Helvath, the Flames' chieftain."

"You don't understand," Dree said, shaking her head. "They'll kill us on sight."

"Maybe not," Lourdvang reasoned.

She looked at him in exasperation. "You were there. They tried to kill us *before* we attacked them and escaped the Teeth. What do you think they'll do now?"

Marcus looked between the two of them. "You did what?"

They were gathered together in the main cavern, Baby Hybrid powered down beside them. Dree was resolute that it wasn't worth going after the Egg, but Marcus and Lourdvang were all for it. Marcus thought it might just be the missing piece they needed, and Lourdvang agreed, though he was at least a bit hesitant about returning to the Teeth.

"Never mind that," Dree snarled. "What would the Egg do anyway?"

Lourdvang was curled up beside them, still eyeing the hybrid thoughtfully. The other dragons in the cavern were watching it as well, though they just looked discomfited. Marcus could understand that: If a mechanical human being was walking around, he'd probably find it unsettling as well.

"It was legend when I heard of it," Lourdvang said. "But Erdath says it exists. He has seen it. It's not a real egg; it's a relic the Flames found in the earth, deep in the caverns of Arncrag. It is said to be what gave the Flames their power. They were not always the greatest of dragons. It gave them their fire."

"And it would work on a machine?" Marcus asked.

"I don't know," he said. "But if it did, the hybrid would be incredibly powerful."

"We need it," Marcus said immediately, turning to Dree. She hesitated. "How are we going to get it?"

"We'll go to the Teeth and ask them to borrow it," Marcus said, shrugging.

Dree just laughed and shook her head. "You're nuts."

"I'm motivated."

Dree hesitated. She definitely didn't like it, but they didn't have a lot of options. She could keep improving the overall design of the hybrid, but they would eventually be limited by simple mechanics. If there was a chance, however slim, of giving the hybrid real dragon magic, they had to take it. With that, it might be able to destroy the drones.

"We should bring Baby Hybrid to show them," Dree said reluctantly.

"I agree," Marcus replied. "Who's going to ride it?"

Dree sighed. "I guess that would be me."

⊕

Dree sat perched on the back of the hybrid, wrapping her hands around the steel plate where the neck protruded up to a dragon's head, its unblinking eyes locked ahead.

Marcus was next to her on Lourdvang, watching. Dree had been the natural choice as the more experienced rider, but they were all worried that the hybrid might drop out of the sky halfway to the Teeth. They needed to test it with a rider though, which is what it was made for: it had limited intelligence, but as a skilled rider, Dree could do the thinking for it. That was the theory, anyway.

"Baby Hybrid," she said tentatively. "Fly."

She felt the strange humming course beneath her legs as the hybrid lifted off the ground. It rose straight up, floating like a dandelion wisp. Dree held on tightly, terrified that the power would short out at any moment and hoping it at least conked out before they got too high. But Baby Hybrid kept climbing, and when she was about ten feet over the exposed ledge, she decided to give it a real test.

"Forward," she said, and the hybrid suddenly rocketed off the ledge.

Dree could barely hold on to the steel plate as it shot

across the sky, and she screamed with fear and excitement—
it was even faster than Lourdvang. She risked a glance back
and saw him trying to catch up. Marcus was pumping his
fist and shouting something.

"All right," Dree said, grinning, "you can move fast.
Let's dive."

The wings adjusted slightly, and the hybrid rocketed
downward.

"Right!" she shouted.

The wings tilted, taking a few seconds again, and then
Baby Hybrid shot to the right, accelerating quickly. It was
far from graceful, but the potential was there. She just needed
to test one more important thing. She had a feeling they
were going to need it.

"Fire machine guns!"

The machines guns were already exposed beneath
each wing, and they immediately loosed a volley of bullets
at a nearby mountain slope. A plume of dust leapt out where
the rocks were incinerated, and Dree laughed and slapped
the hybrid.

"Perfect! Stop firing."

The machine guns went silent.

"Slow down."

Baby Hybrid slowed, allowing Marcus and Lourdvang
to catch up. The hybrid was fast—maybe even faster than
the drones.

"Amazing!" Marcus called, his hands buried into
Lourdvang's scales. "But—"

"It was slow on the turns and dive," Dree admitted. "I know."

"So we go for the Egg."

"Might as well," she said. "Our lives are at stake regardless."

"You're so cheery," Marcus replied, laughing as Lourdvang swept onto another current. Being the only rider on the dragon was an entirely different experience—Marcus almost felt joined with Lourdvang. Of course the dragon clearly still didn't like him, but when they were flying, they settled into an unspoken truce. A small part of him wondered again if he even wanted to go back to Arlington after all this. What was he there? A social pariah that looked at scattered news clippings and played vids with Brian? Here he was a dragon rider. An inventor. How could he go back now?

That was a question for another time. For now, he had to take out the drones, and then he had to find his father. Everything else could wait. But the thought lingered as they turned toward the Teeth.

Dree raced ahead, trying to test the hybrid to its limits. Marcus watched her, shaking his head as she dove into valleys and skimmed treetops, shouting and laughing.

"She's nuts."

"She's reckless," Lourdvang said disapprovingly. "Always has been."

"Because of her brother?"

He grunted. "I think so. She blames herself. But she has a gift, as do you."

"Can I ask you something?"

"You may."

Marcus paused. "Why do I feel like I belong up here?"

Lourdvang turned to look at him. "I suspect it's because you do." He turned back, watching Dree soar just beneath the clouds. "You both do."

They reached the Teeth, and Marcus gazed down with building fear at the jagged, unfriendly landscape. It looked like the mountains had been scorched with fire. There was no sign of life except scraggly clumps of thickets and brambles that bordered the cold stream below, winding through the valley.

"Are we going to be eaten?" he asked, staring at a huge mountain in the distance.

"*You* may be," Lourdvang replied. "Dragons don't eat other dragons."

"That's comforting."

As they approached Arncrag, two crimson dragons—sentries for the lair—leapt off of the peak of a small mountain. They raced toward the trespassers and fell in line beside Lourdvang, clearly unsure of what Baby Hybrid was. They began to rumble and hiss and growl in their language, and Marcus just sat there uneasily while Dree flew a little behind them. The Flames couldn't have known it, but Dree probably had the machine guns trained on their wings. According to Lourdvang, Flames had much tougher wings, but the dual machine guns could still be able to cut through them.

Finally, Lourdvang turned to Marcus. "They will see us."

"That's a start."

"Apparently they have seen the drones, and they are curious. They want answers."

"Did they say they would let us leave after?"

Lourdvang paused. "No."

"Super," Marcus muttered.

They followed the two Flames to Arncrag, bordered by slow-moving clouds catching the sunlight. It looked like the entire mountain was on fire. Dree felt her stomach twisting as she floated beside Marcus and Lourdvang, approaching the dark opening. The last time they had been here, things hadn't gone so well. She fully expected this to go even worse. Their only chance was either Flame mercy or Baby Hybrid's guns.

The odds weren't great either way.

Both Dree and Marcus stayed on their respective mounts as they walked into the cavern. Once again, Helvath sat imperiously on his skull-and-bone dais, a massive, half-eaten carcass below him. It looked like an elk. Vero sat to his right, but the other spot was empty. Dree was happy for that at least. She hadn't liked the eyes of that other dragon.

When he saw them, Helvath started to laugh. It wasn't a pleasant noise. It shook the entire mountain, deep and cold like thunder. His eyes were gleaming.

"You do have a death wish, don't you?" he asked. "You attack me in my own kingdom, flee like rabbits, and then return but a few weeks later to mock me? Not very wise."

"We are not here to mock you," Lourdvang said. "We are here to ask for your help."

"Even stupider," Helvath said. "But I am curious what the lamb asks of the wolf."

"We need the Egg," Dree cut in. "And your warriors."

Helvath turned to her, baring rows of foot-long teeth. Marcus was frozen with fear; Helvath was twice the size of Lourdvang and looked malicious. He suddenly wished he hadn't voted to come here. They would be lucky to leave this mountain alive.

"Really," Helvath said. "What is that . . . thing?"

"Baby Hybrid," Dree said. "Created from one of the drones we destroyed."

Helvath seemed to consider this. "Drones, you call them? Those are the metal objects that fly around the sky like sparrows?"

"Yes. We have to stop them."

"We?" Helvath asked. "They kill humans and lesser dragons. They do my work."

Marcus finally spoke up. "They will turn on you eventually as well."

His voice sounded meek and lonely in the cavern. Helvath turned to him.

"Then we'll destroy them," he growled, narrowing his eyes.

"There will be more," Marcus said. "Now that the drones are here, they may find a way to reopen the portal. If we don't destroy the four left and find a way to close the portal permanently, you may have fifty to deal with. Hundreds, eventually. Even the Flames would perish."

"The machines are deadly," Vero agreed. "I have seen them fight."

Dree wondered if Helvath would just kill them on the spot. His eyes certainly hinted at that very possibility, flicking between them like he couldn't decide who to eat first. She prepared to give Baby Hybrid the order to fire, knowing it would be too late. If Helvath launched a fireball at Lourdvang and Marcus, they would both die instantly.

The silence was heavy as he stared at them. Dree waited for the end.

Instead, he laughed again, shaking the mountain.

"I admire your courage," he said thoughtfully. "I would have thought you would not return here for the rest of your lives. That would have been the wiser choice. And yet you stroll in here again and ask me for help. It is the kind of foolhardy bravery that I have not seen in an age. For that, I will let you live. It is too rare that I see courage in this world these days."

Dree and Marcus exchanged a relieved smile.

"But I will not help you either."

Vero turned to him. "Perhaps we should—"

"I will not send my dragons into a battle to save locusts and worms," Helvath said. "And I would never give them the Egg either. What would you do with it if I did?"

Dree hesitated. "We were going to use it to give this hybrid dragon magic."

Helvath straightened, eyeing the hybrid dangerously. "That seals it, then. You would use our magic on a weapon? My father would return from the ground to burn us all to nothing. I have half a mind to destroy that thing, but I suppose you intend to use it to defeat the drones?"

"Yes," Marcus replied.

"Then go, and if you fail, we will be ready. Hurry before I change my mind and kill the lot of you. Your courage can only go so far before my ceaseless hunger returns."

Marcus, Dree, and Lourdvang slowly exited the cavern. Marcus was disappointed, but Dree was just happy to be alive. They would have to think of something else.

"What now?" Marcus asked.

"We keep working on the hybrid," Dree said. "What else can we do?"

Marcus shook his head. "It's not enough."

"No," a calm voice said. "It's not."

They all looked back in surprise to see Vero following them outside, moving like a stalking cat. She was still bigger than Lourdvang, but sleek and muscled, with the same deadly claws and teeth as Helvath. She also seemed agitated, and they heard Helvath shouting something in the background. Obviously she was not there with his consent.

"He doesn't like when I disobey him," she said, guessing at their thoughts. "But I must speak to you alone. Quickly, before he really does change his mind and decide to attack."

She turned to Lourdvang.

"Do you know of a dragon named Nolong? He is a Sage."

Lourdvang paused. "I don't know the name. I have heard that some Sages have escaped from the dragon hunters and live in secret in these mountains, but I don't know where."

Vero seemed to consider this. "If you ever see him, can you tell him I asked?"

Dree and Marcus looked at each other, confused.

"We . . . knew each other long ago," Vero explained. "In different times. I was forbidden from seeing him—Flames cannot be with other clans. It is considered unseemly. When I heard about the attacks, I wondered if he was among the dead."

"I'll keep an eye out for him," Lourdvang said. "If I see him, I will tell him."

"Thank you," Vero said, nodding her head. "Helvath will never help you. He truly believes the machines are clearing out the countryside of pests, and he will not interrupt their work. He has grown idle and crueler with age, as heartless as the mountain we stand on. But I believe you when you say they will come for us. I have seen them work."

She leaned in, lowering her voice to a rumbling whisper.

"Helvath is a liar. We do not have the Egg."

"What?" Dree blurted out.

"We did, but it was stolen years ago. Have you heard the story of the town of Toloth?"

Dree frowned. "Of course. It was burned to the ground by the Flames."

"Yes," Vero said quietly. "By Helvath himself, in fact. When the Egg was stolen over ten years ago, they followed the trace of it back to Toloth. In his rage, Helvath attacked and destroyed the town, killing everyone. But still he did not find the Egg. We never saw it again."

Marcus and Dree exchanged a disappointed look.

"So the Egg is lost," Dree murmured.

Vero paused. "Perhaps. But I would bet anything that it sits deep in the palace—right beneath your government's watchful gaze. I think they stole it to keep it from us."

"Why do you think that?" Dree asked.

"Because the thief left something behind," Vero said simply. "And I am the one who found it. An empty envelope with a broken wax seal: the royal seal of Dracone. I knew it from the flags on the battlements. The thief must have dropped it."

"Why didn't you tell Helvath?" Marcus asked.

"Because he would have burned the city to the ground in his wrath. He almost did it anyway. I did not know he was headed for Toloth, or I would have tried to stop him from that ill-advised flight as well. I do not share his hatred of other beings. I spared the city for a little while. But if this Egg will help your creation, then go and get it. And please bring it back."

Marcus leaned back on Lourdvang, his mind racing. Who had stolen the Egg? It couldn't have been his father—he hadn't been in Dracone ten years ago. Was it someone from his world, though? Either way, Marcus knew they were getting closer to the truth, and maybe they would find answers in the palace.

"We'll get the Egg," he said, ignoring Dree's exasperated look. "Thank you."

Vero nodded. "Now go . . . and don't return."

With that, she turned and hurried back into the cavern. Lourdvang took off again, and Dree followed on Baby Hybrid. It shuddered and dipped as it ascended after Lourdvang. Dree had to admit, in its current state, the hybrid wouldn't stand a chance against the drones. But the Egg was out of their reach; there was no way they could get into the palace.

"Should we wait for nightfall?" Marcus called over the wind.

"We're not going," Dree said.

"What?"

Baby Hybrid and Lourdvang were flying close together so that Dree and Marcus could shout at each other over the wind.

"It's impossible," she said. "The palace is extremely well guarded."

"You said the same thing about the Teeth," he pointed out.

"Yes, and Helvath could have destroyed us if he wanted to!"

Marcus scowled. "I'm going. I understand if you don't want to."

"You'll be arrested."

"That's fine."

Dree turned to him. "You think your father is in the palace, don't you?"

"He could be," Marcus said.

Dree shook her head. She couldn't blame Marcus for wanting to find his father, but it was no reason to get them all killed. He was going on a hunch and nothing more. Was it worth breaking into the most heavily defended place in Dracone to find something they didn't even know for sure was there? Dree thought about Abi and her brothers, huddling in the cave. She thought of all the other people being attacked in the city. On the other hand, wasn't it worth the risk if there was even a slight chance that the Egg could stop the killing?

If the Egg allowed her to destroy the drones and save her family, then yes. It was a big *if*, but she had to try. There were thousands of other people in danger, and one of them was Abi. Baby Hybrid couldn't save them in its current state. But with the Egg, they had a chance.

"Fine," Dree said, glancing at Lourdvang. "But this time we take—"

She didn't get the chance to finish her thought. Without warning the fire in the hybrid suddenly sputtered and went out, and Baby Hybrid plummeted from the sky.

Chapter 19

Baby Hybrid fell fast, and Dree had to hold on to the steel plate just to keep from slipping off its back. Even then, her fingers were slipping on the metal.

"Baby Hybrid!" Dree screamed. "Power on!"

But nothing happened. It was just a hunk of steel, immobile and lifeless.

Just like Dree was about to become.

Above her, Marcus and Lourdvang had swept into a dive of their own, Lourdvang's wings and legs tucked tightly against his body. Marcus was hugging Lourdvang's neck, trying to stay flat, and a million thoughts were racing through his mind, not the least of which was Dree smashing into the valley below. He must have installed the power cells incorrectly. Maybe the processing core had overheated. He had done this—if Dree died, it was his fault.

"Faster!" he shouted at Lourdvang, already knowing it was impossible.

The hybrid was about two hundred yards from the ground now and falling fast. He saw Dree screaming orders over the wind, trying to restart it. She looked manic, beating the steel with her fist as her hair whipped around and they fell lower.

"Let go!" Marcus called as loudly as he could, knowing she would fall much slower if she spread out her arms and legs and created air resistance.

Dree couldn't hear him, but she already knew that. She just didn't want to let Baby Hybrid fall. It was their chance—it was the one thing she had done to protect her family. If Baby Hybrid was gone, then she had failed them again. She had failed everyone. And even as the ground rushed toward her—a serene valley of ponds and trees and birds that would kill her instantly—she still held on to that hope. A part of her wondered if it was her fate to smash into the ground along with her last chance of redemption.

"Please . . . start!" she pleaded, trying to reach inside the hybrid and trigger the power cells by hand. For just a moment, there was a flicker. But it stayed black.

"Let go!" someone roared. It was Lourdvang. She looked up, feeling tears flood her eyes—either from the cold or the thought of losing the hybrid. She saw Marcus on Lourdvang's back, screaming the same thing, and the tears blurred them together into a shadow chasing her from the past. All of a sudden she saw Gavri, riding on a dark memory.

She saw his strawlike hair in the sun, his eyes as warm as the meadow below. She wanted to say something to him—to apologize, to tell him she loved him, to just weep. But he spoke first.

"Let go."

His voice was calm and gentle. It was the voice of her little brother—so full of wonder. And at once, she knew there would be another chance. That it wasn't over.

She let go of the steel plate and felt herself floating. She turned in midair and opened her legs and arms like Lourdvang had taught her, the wind buffeting her furiously. And through her blurred vision, she felt great claws wrap around her body from above.

Marcus finally relaxed as Lourdvang opened his wings and caught the wind, slowing their terrible fall. They were mere yards from the ground. Then Baby Hybrid hit.

It was bad, but it could have been worse. The valley below was marshy and soft, so Baby Hybrid dug deep into the soil, hitting with a sickening thud instead of a crash. He saw the legs crumple and bend, the wings shatter from their pistons, and the head slap hard into the ground. The entire hybrid seemed to shrink from the impact, but it didn't break.

It wasn't over yet.

Lourdvang landed gently in the marsh, dropping Dree into the spongy grass that reached almost to Lourdvang's knees. Marcus heard desperate cries of birds and beasts as the dragon landed in their midst, and he leapt off of Lourdvang's back and raced to Dree.

She just lay there as Lourdvang stepped back, staring into the sky.

Her face was wet from tears.

Marcus knelt beside her, his hand on her shoulder. He had never even imagined that Dree was capable of crying. He knew it wasn't fear. It was losing the hybrid.

"Are you okay?" he asked gently.

She looked at him and smiled. "I'm fine."

The calm in her voice threw Marcus off. "We were worried you wanted to go down with the ship."

"I thought about it," she said, pushing herself up onto her elbows. "But I changed my mind. How is she?"

Marcus smirked. "She could use a good welder."

"Then we better get to work," Dree said, letting Marcus pull her up.

"If you ever do that again—" Lourdvang growled.

Dree hugged his leg. "I'm sorry, little brother. Thanks for the catch."

Lourdvang just grunted and then nuzzled against her. Dree stayed close to him for a moment, letting his heat spill through her and erase the tears.

"I saw him," she whispered.

Lourdvang didn't need to ask. "And?"

"And he wanted me to stay here."

Lourdvang pulled away and looked at her. "And so do I."

Dree nodded, feeling the tears well again. She quickly turned away, wiping them with her arm. "Let's get Baby Hybrid home."

⊕

It was not an easy trip. Lourdvang struggled terribly with the combined weight of two riders and the hybrid, which he had clutched in his feet. He had to flap constantly to keep them aloft, and Dree whispered encouraging words to him as he struggled through the mountains, keeping low in case he suddenly plummeted from the sky as well.

But Lourdvang made it to Forost, and when he finally set the hybrid down, he immediately collapsed onto the ledge. Dree rushed over to him, and Marcus let them have a moment together. He inspected Baby Hybrid and found that the inner casing of the drone core was still largely intact—particularly the power cells and processor. That meant they could rebuild the frame around it.

But Marcus was definitely concerned—that was twice the hybrid had conked out. And even when it worked, he still questioned if it could stand up to the drones. He was more convinced than ever that they needed the Egg.

"I told you that thing would kill you all," a deep voice grumbled.

Erdath walked out onto the windswept ledge, looking between the damaged hybrid and Lourdvang, who was still trying to push himself to his feet.

"What did they say?" Erdath asked.

Marcus looked away. "They said no. But they don't even have the Egg. They told us where it is."

Erdath frowned. "Where?"

"The palace," Dree replied. "A human stole it years ago."

Erdath seemed to consider this. "And now you want to steal it back."

"We leave tonight," Marcus said firmly.

"Not Lourdvang," Dree cut in, still stroking his forehead. "We're taking Baby Hybrid in—it's not safe for a dragon near the city."

Marcus looked at Baby Hybrid, frowning.

"Clearly I'm going to fix it first," she snapped. "Erdath?"

Erdath sighed deeply, and then he grabbed the hybrid and started pulling it into the cavern. "Humans," he growled. "It was so peaceful without them."

Marcus just smirked and followed him in. He was excited to get back to work.

This time they would get it right.

⊕

Dree worked through the afternoon, repairing the damage and fortifying the hybrid with their leftover scrap metal. Marcus had managed to reposition the power cells, and he even had made some improvements to the wiring, hoping to address the cause of the sudden power outages. He wasn't completely sure, but he thought Baby Hybrid would retain her power for far longer now. He hoped, anyway.

Dree was relentless. Sweat poured over her face like a waterfall, soaking her clothes and keeping her blinking as she welded. They slept for less than an hour.

They did take a small break to join Lourdvang in the main cavern for the naming ceremony for a new young dragon. Dree and Marcus sat in the corner, wrapped in shadows as the gathering of dragons hummed and sang and growled in their own language. In the middle of the circle was a young Nightwing, about the size of an elephant and pitch-black, looking small and scared at all the attention.

Lourdvang was close, translating once in a while.

"What's happening?" Dree asked.

"They're telling a story of the first Nightwings," Lourdvang said, watching the ceremony closely. He listened for a moment. When he spoke again, it was almost in tune, low and gravelly but strangely soothing. "They came from the earth and shadows," he started. "Flying in the great depths below. But when they emerged from the mountains they saw the stars like fire in the deep, and they knew they had finally come home."

Dree and Marcus listened, pressed together against the rock wall.

"They dug into Forost and roamed the skies, finding beasts and birds and other dragons that came from forests and fire and the stars. One day they found man, and friends they became, brothers and sisters that rode together on the northern wind."

As they watched, Erdath stood over the young dragon and blew out a smoky shape—a dragon fully formed—and then breathed fire into the smoke to light it up. The dragons sang louder, and Erdath seemed to grow over them like the mountain itself.

"In time the Nightwings grew far and wide, and the young were born under the stars, under shadow and power. And to you, young one, we call you to the clan. You live with your kin, you fly with your kin, you die with your kin. Will you answer the call?"

The young dragon rumbled, and the crowd shook with excitement.

Erdath stood taller and growled something. Songs and shouts filled the room like an orchestra gone mad.

"Then I name you Windrin," Lourdvang said quietly. "May you fly far."

Dree and Marcus watched as the celebration began, and Marcus was left thinking about how these dragons had a culture and beliefs and families, and how wrong it was that the humans in Dracone had turned on them. Part of him wanted to protect the dragons most of all.

They walked back to their side cavern in silence, both lost to their thoughts.

The next day there was only welding work to be done, so Marcus and Lourdvang just watched over Dree as she worked. Finally, after growing more and more agitated with the extra eyes on her, she turned to them.

"Why don't you give Marcus some flying lessons?" she

said to Lourdvang. "If we're going into battle, you better make sure he knows how to stay on your back."

Marcus looked at Lourdvang hopefully, and he nodded. "Very well."

Soon they were high over the mountains, soaring in and out of the clouds and laughing uproariously as Lourdvang sent them into occasional dives.

"Ready to try a corkscrew?" Lourdvang asked, glancing back.

Marcus hunched down and gripped his scales tightly. "Let's do it."

Lourdvang immediately sent them spinning through the air, diving at the same time. The clouds and mountains rolled over Marcus's head in a blur, and he felt incredible g-forces pulling at his body from all directions. He shouted with delight as Lourdvang straightened again, catching a current and gently sailing upward into the clouds.

Marcus felt incredibly free up in the air—the world was small below, and so were its many problems. In the sky, he didn't have to think about what he looked like or what other people thought about him or even about his endless search for his father. There were only air and sun and clouds— only peace.

"So there are no dragons where you come from?" Lourdvang asked.

"No," Marcus replied. "We have planes—kind of like the drones, but some are as big as Flames, and hundreds of people ride on them across the globe."

Lourdvang turned to look at him. "I would like to see such a thing."

Marcus laughed. "I think it might cause a panic if you showed up in my world."

"What do you do in your world?"

"I'm a student. Well, most of the time. Other than that I kind of just looked for my dad."

"You said he disappeared when you were young?"

"Yes. I believe he came here, but I don't know where."

Lourdvang grunted. "My parents left me when I was a baby. I do not remember them. Not much, anyway. I remember something standing over me—something large and warm. I remember sadness, and then nothing. Even as a baby, I thought I was going to die. Dragons grow faster than humans, and we start with a more developed mind. Part of survival. But we are not independent. I needed help to survive."

"And then Dree found you."

"Yes. She was just a little girl herself, but she cared for me. She spent every day with me in the cave, bringing me milk and whatever scraps she could manage from the city. I grew quickly, and soon I could hunt rabbits and birds and squirrels. But I was still alone, and Dree became everything for me. My whole world. Even as I grew, she was my big sister. She will always be that to me, and I will protect her at any cost."

Marcus heard the emotion in Lourdvang's voice. Lourdvang had thought he'd lost her.

"Do you ever think about your parents?" Marcus asked.

"Always," he said. "But they made their own paths, and I must make mine."

Marcus thought about that for a while as they soared over the edge of the mountains. The city was visible in the distance. Over the past week, the drones had leveled much of it, though the downtown core was still intact. Smoking ruins covered the outer ring, and Marcus spotted a Tracker far in the distance, watching over the devastation.

"You must be angry that I brought them here," Marcus said.

"I was," Lourdvang replied. "But I know now you want to destroy them. I am angry with the people who sent them. They kill humans and dragons alike, and they must pay. I think our only chance to stop them is if the three of us work together."

Marcus nodded. "Should we go check on Dree?"

"She is probably enjoying the peace and quiet," Lourdvang chuckled, his eyes on his secret cave below, where Dree's family was sheltering from the drones. There were scattered clothes drying in the sun. "But she'll be happy to know her family is fine."

They circled back toward Forost, the midday sun burning brightly over a lush, magical world of soldiers, dragons, and castles. It all seemed so real to Marcus—even more real than the world he had left. Arlington was starting to feel like a dream, far away and fading.

The thought disturbed him, but he didn't have much time think about it.

He had a palace to break into, and a world to save.

Chapter 20

Dree gingerly put down the welding torch, her hands throbbing and calloused from hours of work. She had barely let go of the torch for two days, working endlessly on Baby Hybrid. Her eyes were dry and sore from welder's blindness—a common symptom of staring at a blazing hot flame all day and night. She was generally more immune to it than most, but working so many hours in the dark cavern had pushed her tolerance to the limit. She stepped back and wavered a little, exhausted.

Despite all that, she was very pleased. The hybrid had been completely salvaged, and she had even improved it: new armored plating on the wing joints, better flexibility on the legs, and an enhanced mouth mechanism. Baby Hybrid could bite now and release limited fire from her gullet. It was closer to being a dragon than before, but it still needed help to become a true weapon. Dree didn't know exactly what the Egg could do, but if it gave Baby Hybrid dragon magic, it was worth the risk. Still, she was very proud of what she had done—the hybrid was magnificent.

What was more, for the first time in her life, she hadn't had any flashbacks. No images of burning hallways or screaming, even in the brief naps she had taken. Gavri wasn't there anymore, calling for her to help him. He was happy, riding somewhere on the back of a dragon, and he had told her to move on. To live her life. It was like she had finally gotten to say goodbye, and she looked at the world in a new light.

Now she just had to make sure it wasn't destroyed.

"All set," Marcus called from where he was sitting in the corner.

"What's set?" Dree asked.

Marcus rubbed his hands together eagerly. "I programmed a homing beacon in Baby Hybrid. If I try to place a call from my cell, she will recognize the signal and find us immediately."

"Impressive," Dree said.

"At least we'll have a little backup if things go wrong in the palace," he replied. "Now I just need to figure out how to turn Lourdvang's fire into a power source. Still working on that one. How's Baby Hybrid?"

"She's ready," Dree said, running her hands over Baby Hybrid's snout.

Marcus grinned and climbed to his feet. Lourdvang was sleeping in the corner.

"It looks great," Marcus said admiringly. "You have the touch."

"I do try," Dree replied. "I'm going to take her for a test spin."

Marcus turned to Lourdvang. "I'll get—"

"No," she said. "Let him sleep. He'll need it."

"What if the hybrid conks out?"

She shook her head. "It won't. Not this time. We did everything right. I also made a new addition: two shafts leading to her heart. If she loses power, I can send some fire of my own to kick-start her again."

"Brilliant," Marcus said. "Want me to come?"

"No," she replied. "I want to really stretch her legs this time."

He laughed. "Okay. But be careful. She'll come right back here if there's trouble, so make sure you're on board."

"Will do." Dree turned to him, meeting his eyes. "Thank you for helping us with all this. I know you want to be out there searching for your father."

"Saving Dracone is my responsibility," he said. "There's nowhere I'd rather be."

There was a moment of awkward silence, and then Dree looked away. "This is going to be bad . . . fighting the drones. Are you ready for war?"

"Not even close," he admitted. "I feel faint just thinking about it."

Dree laughed. "I know exactly you what you mean."

She climbed on board the hybrid.

"Baby Hybrid," she said. "Fly."

Marcus watched as she raced out of the cavern, and then he went back to his laptop to see if he could find a way to get it working.

Outside, Dree was already hundreds of feet away, screaming across the sky. Today she was really going to push Baby Hybrid—she wanted to know exactly what it could do.

"Top speed!" she shouted, and the hybrid accelerated even faster.

She barely held on, her strong fingers clenching the steel plate. Baby Hybrid was incredibly fast. The mountains whizzed past beneath them, and Dree grinned.

"Dive!" she shouted, ducking low in preparation.

Baby Hybrid tilted its wings and sent them shooting downward, still slow but better than before. It turned and fired more effectively, and she laughed as it blew a massive boulder apart before turning and climbing back into the sky. The hybrid was definitely much improved, and Dree suspected that it might even be able to take on a drone. But four of them—there was still no chance. Not without the dragons' help.

She streaked over the last western mountain by the city, where her family was huddled in Lourdvang's secret cave. She thought about going down to see them, but she was afraid the hybrid might attract unwanted attention. If there were any drones in the area, they might investigate. For now, the safest thing was to leave her family alone.

Seeing no drones over the city, she made her way to the south end, low enough that she could see the destruction. As she passed over the docks, her stomach sank. The homes in her neighborhood were completely leveled—nothing but heaps of charred, smoking wood. Her house was gone, as was Mrs. Warmen's. Dree felt sick as she stared at the rubble.

Dree couldn't resist investigating. Her designs had been in the house. If they had survived the attack, she wanted them back.

"Baby Hybrid," she said. "Land."

The forward engines immediately stopped, and they started dropping downward in a controlled, steady descent. They touched down on the street in front of her house, and Dree leapt off of the hybrid's back. The docks were completely deserted. The area was in absolute ruins. Not a single house was standing in a half-mile radius. She felt her knees wobble as she looked out over the neighborhood she had grown up in. Streets she had played in, houses she had visited, people she had known. They were all gone. Glass littered the streets. Clothes and personal possessions were scattered everywhere—once-priceless things to a peasant that meant nothing in death.

It was all gone. She slowly stepped up onto the pile of debris that had been her home, pulling planks of wood and roof slats off, looking for the memories beneath. She found her father's armchair, mostly burned but still sitting in the same place. She half expected him to be sitting in it. She found the charred frame for one of her mother's prized pictures—the image itself burned away. Pots and pans. A kitchen chair. Her little brothers' cots, still standing next to each other but with the blankets scorched to ashes.

Dree finally found her room in the rubble. Her cot was nothing but a blackened frame. She wanted to cry at the sight, but her tears had already emptied in the meadow. These were just things, and they could get more. Her family was safe, and that was all that really mattered. She pawed beneath the bed and finally found the small figurine of the dragon and its rider. Despite the fire and destruction, it remained.

Just like her and Lourdvang.

At least it was something. A memory that hadn't been completely destroyed.

Dree was just turning to go when a flash of movement caught her eye. She scooped up a chunk of wood by instinct, ready to fight, but it was too late. In an instant, five spears were held to her stomach and throat, wielded by grim-faced soldiers. Their chest plates were marked with a red flame, and their helmets were arched and curved over their cheeks. Each man was at least six feet tall and very muscular.

The Prime Minister's personal guard—the deadliest soldiers in Dracone.

Five more were slowly approaching Baby Hybrid, looking cautious. She understood: they had seen her land here, and they wanted to know what the hybrid was. They would take it back to the palace, and she would never see it again.

"Baby Hybrid," she shouted, "go back to the mountain!"

The hybrid reacted instantly. It shot into the air, avoiding the many iron spears hurled at it, and then shot toward the mountains in a flash. Dree grinned as it disappeared.

The Prime Minister wasn't going to get Baby Hybrid. Not if she could help it.

The lead soldier, a tall man with a black beard and hard eyes, turned to her. "That was not wise," he snarled, and then he punched her right in the chin with a gauntleted right fist.

Dree didn't even see it coming. She just felt herself falling, and then there was darkness.

Chapter 21

Marcus pumped his fist in excitement as the laptop suddenly turned on. He had managed to rig up a small power cell with leftover parts from the drone, but it still hadn't worked—not until he gently put his finger on the cell, making sure Lourdvang wasn't watching—and let the fire out. Usually it happened only when he was angry and not in control, but this time he just let it happen, and suddenly a scarlet flame snaked its way down his finger and into the power cell. As soon as it did, the laptop began charging. It confirmed Marcus's growing suspicion: The fire that he and Dree possessed was very similar to the power in Lourdvang—not just fire, but energy.

It didn't make sense in the traditional notion of physics,

but it explained a lot about the dragons. The fire was their energy, keeping them aloft and never burning out. It wasn't just physics—it was magic. Or at least some combination of the two. As a science buff, he was reluctant to accept that physics couldn't explain everything. As a kid sitting in a lair with a dragon, he was more open to the possibilities.

But why could he create the fire? Did his father have the same ability?

There was so much he didn't know about his family. A father who had left him at four years old, and a mother he had never met. He thought back to the only discussion he'd ever had about his mother.

He had walked into the living room, where Jack was sitting on the couch. Jack would usually get home at nine, plop down, and watch TV until ten. He left Marcus money to buy pizzas or takeout or ready-made stuff from the grocery store, and Marcus always just left extra for him. He was the only ten-year-old he knew doing the grocery shopping.

This time Marcus was holding a photo album, the only one he had.

Jack saw it and smiled faintly, as if he knew what was coming. He took a sip of beer and kept his eyes on the TV.

"Can I ask you something?"

"You may," he said quietly.

"Why are there no pictures of my mom?"

Jack was silent for a long moment. "Sit down."

Marcus sat down next to him, the photo album in his lap.

"When I met your dad, your mother had already died,"

he said, his eyes still on the TV. Jack wasn't a very affection-
ate person. He didn't hug or clap shoulders or even make eye
contact for long. "Even I don't know how. He told me once
that she was a warrior, and that I would have liked her. I'm
not sure if he meant she was a soldier, or perhaps that she
had fought for her life. He didn't say, and I didn't want to
ask. In fact, I never saw a picture of her either."

Marcus frowned. "But why don't we have any?"

"Your dad didn't talk about her much, but when he
did . . . I knew it was still painful. It was more than mourning,
I think . . . almost as if he felt guilty for her death. It's a normal thing. We all want to protect the ones we love, and if we
can't, we blame ourselves. I think he destroyed the pictures.
Her clothes and possessions. He got rid of everything when
he moved here, trying to leave the memories behind him."

"Does that work?" Marcus murmured.

Jack paused. "Not for him."

Marcus still remembered going back to his room with
his photo album, wondering what his mother had looked
like. Over time he had stopped wondering; he figured he
would never know. But now that he was closer to his father,
he wanted to know the truth.

For the moment, though, he was in a cave with a dragon,
he had just turned on a computer with his fingers, and he
was waiting for a girl to return on her flying dragon hybrid.

He watched as his operating system opened, and he
thought about what Brian would say if he could see all this.
He was fairly sure his best friend would faint when he first

saw Lourdvang, but he would be absolutely ecstatic to be in a world of swords and magic. Brian was an even bigger fantasy nerd than Marcus. Marcus wished he could bring him here, even for a day. Of course Brian would probably also swoon over Dree and break out in hives, so maybe it was for the best.

Marcus smiled and opened his coding program, figuring he might as well work on Baby Hybrid's programming while Dree was gone.

He was just starting when Baby Hybrid raced into the cavern, settling into the middle of the room and waiting. Marcus looked up to say hello and then pushed his laptop aside. He jumped to his feet, feeling his stomach flip. Dree wasn't there.

"Lourdvang!" he shouted, racing over to Baby Hybrid.

"What?" he rumbled, opening one blue eye.

"She's gone."

Lourdvang was up in an instant, smoke roiling from his nose. "Gone where?"

"She took the drone out for a test. . . . She didn't come back."

Lourdvang started for the opening, obviously going after her.

"Wait!" Marcus called. "We need Baby Hybrid."

He leapt up onto its back and grabbed the steel plate.

"Take us back to where you were," he ordered. "Now!"

Baby Hybrid immediately flew out of the cavern again, Lourdvang following after it. They shot into the air, and Marcus had to tell it to slow down a little so that Lourdvang could keep up. Lourdvang was in a rage though, and he was flying fast. They raced over the mountains, and Marcus realized that they were heading for the city. Had she gone to visit her parents in the cave? Had she actually landed in the city? Had the drones picked her off before she could get there? They wouldn't know until Baby Hybrid stopped.

Marcus felt his insides churning at the thought of Dree being killed. His hands were trembling on the steel, and he felt a terrible heat racing through him. Why had he let her go by herself? He should have gone with her, or at least woken up Lourdvang to follow her. Now she was gone.

They reached the last mountain, where Dree's family was hidden, but Baby Hybrid kept flying. She hadn't seen her family—she was too smart to expose them like that. But where had she gone?

They flew out over the city, and Marcus anxiously scanned the horizon for drones. Nothing. If they had been here, they were long gone by now.

The ruined city passed below them, and then Baby Hybrid abruptly stopped and started to descend. Marcus looked down, trying to figure out why she had come here. It took him a moment to recognize where they were—the docks. She had come back to her home. Or what was left of it. The entire area was rubble. Her house had been wiped away like sand. Lourdvang descended right beside him, scanning the area for Dree.

"She must have landed," Marcus called. "I'll look for her—"

He stopped as something caught his eye. A glint of sunlight.

Marcus leaned over the hybrid, narrowing his eyes. And then he saw them. Two men huddled against one of the ruined houses, spears in hand. Then he saw ten more close by, all taking shelter and waiting. Soldiers.

"Pull up!" he shouted desperately.

Lourdvang looked at him. "We have to—"

"Now!" he said. "Baby Hybrid . . . go up!"

The soldiers realized what was happening almost instantly. They stepped out from cover and started throwing spears and unleashing crossbow bolts. Lourdvang roared as a barbed arrow ripped through the membrane on his right wing. He swept upward, Baby Hybrid racing after him. Marcus heard an arrow hit the iron hull, falling away uselessly. They ascended far out of range, and Marcus turned to Lourdvang.

"Are you all right?" he asked worriedly.

"Fine," Lourdvang growled. "I should kill them all."

"I wouldn't argue," Marcus said. "Let's go land somewhere. We need to figure this out."

They landed soon after, up on the summit of a great mountain. Marcus looked at Lourdvang's injured wing in concern as he landed in the snow, sending a shower of steam billowing into the air. The hole was small enough that it didn't affect his flight, but it looked painful. Lourdvang dunked his wing in the snow, sighing as the steam shot out.

"They must have taken her," Marcus said. "The soldiers. Who are they?"

"The Prime Minister's personal guard," Lourdvang explained. "The Protectorate. They are the only soldiers who wear full fire-resistant armor. They specialize in dragon killing."

"They must have seen Baby Hybrid and taken Dree for questioning," Marcus said.

Lourdvang growled, shooting black smoke into the air. "Why did she have to land? Why didn't she tell me she was going? If they hurt her I'll burn that palace—"

"The drones will take care of that," Marcus muttered. "Is that where they take prisoners?"

Lourdvang paused. "No. Dree told me of another place. Ancient dragon caves in one of the nearby mountains to the north. She said they had converted them into a prison some years ago. Supposedly impenetrable."

"Great."

"But they are dragon caves," Lourdvang said, "stolen from my people. There is always more than one entrance. I bet the humans have not found them all."

Marcus turned to him. "Time for a jailbreak."

Chapter 22

ree woke up to torchlight flickering and dancing in her vision. Her head was pounding.

She tried to move but found that her arms were firmly strapped to a table with leather cuffs, and though she struggled, she couldn't yank them out. Her waist was bound, as were her legs. She was tilted forward, staring at a rock wall veined with white granite, like spiderwebs. She suddenly remembered the soldier and the fist connecting with her jaw.

She instantly knew where she was. The Cave Prisons. Which meant she might as well stop struggling—no one escaped these caves. There was supposedly only one way in and one way out. She wondered if Marcus and Lourdvang would ever find her here.

She doubted it.

"You're awake," a cool voice said.

A woman wearing fire-resistant armor stepped in front of Dree, her short golden hair tied back into a bun. She obviously didn't bother with the new fashions: she was a soldier, through and through. She looked at Dree like she was some sort of vermin.

"Why did you take me here?" Dree asked, her voice hoarse and croaking. She was very thirsty, and she wondered how long she'd been strapped to the hard, cold table.

"We have some questions," the woman said, smiling. It was an unpleasant smile. "My name is Lieutenant Alva. I specialize in . . . getting answers."

She let the threat hang in the air. Dree understood. She was a torturer.

Alva leaned in, taking Dree's chin in her hands. "What was that machine?"

"What machine?" Dree asked, meeting her gaze.

Alva dug her fingers into Dree's skin. "The one you were riding on."

Dree felt blood running down her chin. The woman dug her nails in even deeper.

"It was a dragon," she said tersely. "Not a machine."

Alva smiled again. She had sparkling white teeth. Without warning, she slapped Dree across the face with the back of her hand. Dree gasped under the blow.

"Don't lie to me, girl," she said. "I hate liars. They don't leave these caves."

"Does the Prime Minister know you're torturing an innocent subject?"

"The Prime Minister lets us do what we must to protect Dracone," she snarled.

Dree met her eyes. "Then why not go after those drones instead?"

Lieutenant Alva's expression flickered for just a moment—something like doubt.

"What was the machine?" she asked again, her voice low.

"It was a bat," Dree said. "A really big one."

Lieutenant Alva smirked and cracked her knuckles. Then the beating began.

⊕

"Is that it?" Marcus called to Lourdvang, who was flying beside Baby Hybrid.

They were high above a squat gray mountain to the immediate north of the city. Marcus could make out a large regiment of soldiers at its base, standing in front of a heavily fortified opening in the stone. Even from there it looked completely impassable.

"Yes," Lourdvang replied, gliding in a circle like a vulture. "It was once used by the Nightwings—the ones who partnered with riders. They could stay close there."

"Makes sense," Marcus mused. "So how do we get in?"

Lourdvang was still scanning the mountain. Far below, Marcus could see the soldiers readying themselves. They had seen Lourdvang circling overhead and were already wheeling catapults and lances forward.

"The entrance the humans use was for the riders," Lourdvang said. "The dragons used other entrances that were more accessible from the sky. We just have to find them."

They circled the mountain for a while, searching desperately for another cave opening. Finally, Lourdvang spotted one. There was just one problem: it had been sealed.

"So they did find them," Lourdvang said, as Marcus flew over to him.

Marcus examined the entrance. It had been sealed with concrete and brick, almost matching the dull gray color of the mountain. It was unguarded, of course, but it was probably two feet thick.

Lourdvang looked at him. "We'll just have to try and storm the entrance."

"No. I think we should use this one."

"I can't break through brick," Lourdvang said. "Even fire will not—"

"Who said you had to do it?" Marcus asked, patting the hybrid lovingly. "Baby Hybrid, lock on the concrete wall up there with your missiles."

He heard whirring beneath him as a missile emerged from the hybrid's body.

Marcus grinned. "Fire."

Dree slammed into the hard stone floor of the cell, pain racing through her bruised body. Alva had been merciless:

pummelling her stomach and arms and face continually until Dree was just hanging there like a marionette. Dree was now a mess of bruises and cuts, but she still hadn't said a word about the hybrid. She knew Alva would use the information to set a trap for Marcus and Lourdvang. The government would want the weapon.

Dree slowly pushed herself into a crouch and huddled against the wall. The cell was barely ten feet by ten feet, with a bucket in the corner that smelled like fetid urine and worse. The bars were heavy iron, and the only light was from a torch down the hall.

So much for the Prime Minister's promises of a bright future and human rights and transparent government. It had sounded great to most Draconians, but they didn't know the truth. The government was using this hole to keep prisoners without a trial or even charges. They were torturing their own citizens.

She crawled over to the bars and looked down the tunnel. It was lined with cells like hers, and she thought she saw some dark shadows lurking behind the bars. If they were humans, they had been held captive far too long.

"What did you do?" a quiet female voice asked.

Dree jerked. "Who's there?"

"Your new neighbor," the voice said sadly. "They treated you even worse than usual. What did you do?"

"Nothing," Dree said bitterly. "I tried to help fight the drones."

The woman laughed. "Then I understand."

"What do you mean?"

"I've only been here for a week. It feels like a year. I was a community leader. I spoke out about the fact that the government still hadn't sent troops to find the machines. They even started landing in the city—setting up a base on the outskirts. Our soldiers still didn't attack, even when the drones were parked right within striking distance."

"Why?" Dree asked, astounded that the drones even left themselves open to attack.

"That was my question. Meanwhile, the dragon hunters are still working."

Dree tried to make sense of what she was hearing. "But the drones are destroying the city."

"Parts of it, yes," the voice said. "My neighborhood included. When I spoke up and tried to get the word to the people, they snatched me in the night. I woke up here."

Dree leaned back again, her mind racing. Francis was beloved by everyone—he'd turned the city around and done everything he could to expand it. Why would he possibly allow it to be destroyed now? Why would he not attack the drones if they had landed?

"I don't understand it either," the woman said. "But I don't think it's our problem anymore."

"Maybe," Dree whispered, thinking of Marcus and Lourdvang. "But I still—"

She was cut off by a massive boom that shook the entire mountain and raced down the tunnels like a thunderbolt. Dree immediately jumped to her feet, grabbing onto the bars for support. Were the drones attacking?

And then a deafening roar followed the explosion—one she knew very well.

Lourdvang.

Soldiers rushed past her cell, and a few moments later, they came running back down the tunnel again, looking panicked. There were fewer than before. Suddenly the tunnel lit up with fire, and she heard loud, stomping feet rushing down the cavern.

"Dree!" Marcus called.

"Here!" she called out. "I'm down here."

Lourdvang appeared in front of the cell, hunched down in the tunnel. His eyes flashed dangerously when he saw her, and then he tore the bars from the wall.

"Who?" he growled.

"Never mind," Dree said. "Let's go."

Marcus was right behind Lourdvang, riding Baby Hybrid. He had the machine guns trained down the tunnel. Dree leapt up onto Lourdvang's back and looked at the cell next to her. An older woman was huddled against the bars, watching in amazement.

"You sure you didn't do anything?" she asked, smiling.

"Stand back," Dree ordered.

The woman did as she was told, and Lourdvang ripped her cell bars off as well. She stepped out, moving gingerly. "Thank you, dear," she said. "I'm Ellie, by the way."

"Hop on, Ellie," Marcus said, and she climbed up on the hybrid. "Let's go."

They hurried back through the cavern again, which veered up toward a jagged hole that had been blown into the side of the mountain. Baby Hybrid flew right through the opening and into the sky, and Ellie squealed with delight and fear, hugging Marcus.

Dree and Lourdvang leapt into the air after them.

"Do you want to come with us?" Marcus asked Ellie, glancing back.

"Set me down somewhere if you can," she said. "I need to find my family."

He nodded and found a place on the outskirts of the city to drop her off.

Ellie waved to Dree and jumped off. "Go get those drones," she said to Marcus, meeting his eyes. "No one else is."

As Ellie disappeared into the city, Marcus rejoined Dree and Lourdvang in the clouds. He saw soldiers pouring out of the cave prisons, but they were much too late. Marcus grinned as he flew beside Lourdvang, and then the smile immediately slipped from his face when he saw the bruises and cuts lining Dree's body.

"What did they do—"

"It's nothing," she said, turning away. "We need to get back to see Erdath."

"Why?"

She turned to the city.

"Because I'm not so sure that humans are the real target of the drones. There's a reason the palace is still standing. I think they are coming for the dragons next."

Chapter 23

Marcus and Dree stood before Erdath once again, Lourdvang and Baby Hybrid close behind them. Dree finished relaying what Ellie had told her and outlined her suspicions that the Prime Minister and his government might not be completely innocent in the conflict. If they weren't attacking the drones, they might very well be allied with them.

"If this is true, why destroy so much of the city?" Erdath asked.

"The drones destroyed the poor districts," Dree explained. "The outside towns and villages. They never touched the downtown core or the palace. The new Dracone is completely intact."

Marcus looked at her, still reeling from the information. He'd been so sure that the drones were sent by his government to wipe out everything in Dracone. The news that the Prime Minister and his cabinet might have a connection was tough to believe. But the facts were there: If the drones were landing in the city and the soldiers weren't even bothering to attack them, something nefarious was going on.

Erdath looked out over the assembled dragons, rising to his full height. "They have killed many dragons already," he said thoughtfully. "More and more every day. Some say the Outliers have almost been purged from these mountains. Once they are done with them, they may turn to us." He looked at Dree. "What would you have us do?"

Dree met his eyes, her body still throbbing with pain. She was covered in so many bruises that it hurt to move. But she was angry—angrier than she had ever been in her life. If the government of Dracone had a part in this, then she wanted revenge. Now.

"Nothing yet," she said, trying to keep calm. Her hands were clenching at her sides, the fire threatening to erupt. "Marcus and I are still going to try and get the Egg. If it works, Baby Hybrid might be able to wipe out the drones herself. But if we fail, then the dragons have to be ready. You must gather your kind together—all of them—and be ready to fight. If the dragons from your clan and nearby ones join together, you may have a chance."

Erdath shook his head. "We are not friendly with dragons of other clans. We have never fought together."

"Well, now would be a good time to start," Marcus said.

Erdath may have been stubborn, but he understood

what needed to be done. "Very well. I will send envoys. But I do not have much faith in their success. Regardless, our clan will be ready. Good luck in your quest."

Marcus and Dree nodded and started for the side cavern to rest and plan for the night's attack. Dree wanted to leave immediately, but she knew they would never make it into the palace without the cover of darkness. The city was almost certainly on high alert after their attack on the prison, and they both knew it wasn't going to be easy to get to the palace regardless.

Marcus and Dree dropped onto the ground while Lourdvang nestled in the corner, curling into a ball. Baby Hybrid parked itself in the middle of the room and powered down.

"This should be fun tonight," Marcus said, sighing.

"Yeah," she replied, lying back and wincing. "Ow."

"They really took it to you," Marcus said, looking over her bruised arms. "Were they asking about the hybrid?"

"Yeah. She seemed keener on the hitting part, though."

"Want me to get you some snow or something?"

She laughed, feeling her ribs ache. "That's all right. Some sleep would be nice."

"Well, you can have a few hours of that," he said. "That's it, I'm afraid. We should probably get close before sundown and then go in on foot."

"Agreed," Dree said. "But first, sleep."

"First sleep," he said, lying down beside her. "We were worried about you."

"I was stupid," she said. "Landing in the city."

Marcus paused, looking at her. "I saw your house."

"You mean the pile of rubble that was my house," she corrected.

"Yeah. I'm . . . so sorry."

Dree turned and looked at him, hearing the guilt in his voice.

"Listen," she said, "this isn't your fault. The more I learn, the more I realize that there are lots of other people to blame. You came to find your dad. You meant no harm. And if the Prime Minister is involved in all of this, the drones would have gotten here one way or the other. Okay?"

"Okay," Marcus said, surprised. "Thanks."

Dree smiled. "Sometimes we just need to let go."

She closed her eyes again, but she took his hand and squeezed it.

"You seem different," he said.

"More bruised, you mean?" she asked softly.

"More wise."

Dree glanced at him. "Maybe. But also more angry. Now get some sleep."

She closed her eyes again and dozed off, and Marcus watched her for a moment. He lay back, staring up at the stalactites that loomed threateningly over his head. He kept his hand in hers, appreciating the warmth. He fell asleep wondering about George Brimley and where he fit into all this.

Marcus and Dree sat together on Baby Hybrid, his hands wrapped around her waist once more. Dree had her pack, containing a welding torch and small fuel tank to power it, wrapped over her shoulders. She had come up with the plan a few hours earlier: She had once seen sewer and water systems running into the side of the palace, protected by iron grates that stopped anyone from following them. But with her torch, she might just be able to weaken the steel enough to open the grates and get inside. It was risky, but it was the only way.

Lourdvang was watching in disapproval—Dree had told him he couldn't come. It would be quieter on the hybrid and less dangerous if it needed to come to their rescue. And if dragons were the real target of the drones, then Lourdvang didn't need to be sitting out in the open waiting for them.

"I still think it would be better to have me nearby—" he grumbled.

"They are right," Erdath cut in, standing beside him on the ledge. "It's better this way."

Lourdvang glared at Erdath but didn't argue.

Erdath turned to Dree. "If you get the Egg, you will know what to do. I will prepare our forces here. Either way, we should be ready for battle in a few days."

Dree nodded. "Thank you. Lourdvang—stop looking at me like that."

"No," Lourdvang said, pouting. "This is too dangerous."

"It's all too dangerous," Dree replied sadly. "We have no choice."

"I would come at the city from the north," Erdath said. "The tall mountains there block the horizon. You will have to cross the Gully, and you can even use it to get close to the city without being seen by man or drone. That is the path I would take."

"The Gully?" Marcus asked.

Dree smiled. "You'll know it when you see it. Baby Hybrid, fly."

The hybrid shot upward, and Dree waved down at Lourdvang, feeling guilty. She didn't want to leave him here, but it was much safer for him to stay. She knew he felt like she was replacing him with the hybrid, but she was just more willing to risk the hybrid than her little brother. She hoped he understood that.

"I wish we had some weapons," Dree mused.

Marcus glanced at her. "Do you know how to use a sword?"

She snorted. "I made them for three years. Do you?"

"Only in video games." He noticed Dree's confused look. "Never mind."

They flew north over the mountains, the setting sun glowing on the western horizon, cresting the peaks with gold. It was a calm night, and the few clouds that dotted the sky seemed to hang there like orange blossoms. Bird calls filled the air.

"It's a beautiful land," Marcus commented.

"It is," Dree agreed. "My people forgot about that. They just saw resources to be stolen."

"They aren't alone in that," Marcus replied, thinking of his home.

They flew for about fifteen minutes when Marcus suddenly looked down and gasped. Dree had said he would know the Gully when he saw it, and she was definitely right.

It was a canyon, but it was more spectacular than anything he had ever seen. Jack had taken him to the Grand Canyon when he was younger, and he had stared out in absolute wonder. The Gully made the Grand Canyon look like a crack in the sidewalk. It was at least ten times larger, stretching many miles across and probably five miles deep, splitting the mountain range in two. A river ran far below, looking tiny in the distance. The canyon walls were steep and jagged and pockmarked with endless nooks and ledges, like a honeycomb. It was a staggering thing to behold, and Marcus just stared at it, speechless.

"I told you," Dree said. "I remember when Lourdvang first took me here."

"It's so . . . big."

She laughed. "Yeah. That river down there is huge, if you can believe it."

"I can't," Marcus said. "Let's check it out—"

He stopped as something caught his eye. There, approaching rapidly from the city, were two Trackers, followed by a white Destroyer. They were speeding toward them in an arrow point. "Uh-oh."

Dree saw them immediately. "Baby Hybrid . . . dive!"

The hybrid instantly dove into the canyon, falling beneath the surface and streaking down the mile-high walls toward the river. The sand-hued rock sped past in a blur, and Dree and Marcus held on tightly as they plummeted downward.

"Baby Hybrid, straighten out," Dree ordered, leveling them off.

Marcus looked up and saw the three drones drop into the canyon overhead.

"We still have company."

"Go!" Dree ordered, and Baby Hybrid leapt forward, racing through the canyon.

The drones weren't taking any chances this time. They opened fire.

Marcus shouted in terror as bullets erupted into the river and shoreline behind them, the sound echoing through the canyon. Baby Hybrid shot forward at full speed, right over the turbulent river that crashed against the rocks in massive white-water swells that were at least ten feet high. Baby Hybrid weaved around one, avoiding the violent wave.

Marcus looked back and saw the drones falling behind—the hybrid was faster.

"I think we're losing them—"

The words were barely out of his mouth when two more Trackers dropped into the canyon in front of them, moving fast. They opened fire, and the river erupted with twin streams of machine gun fire that raced toward Baby Hybrid.

"Hold on!" Dree screamed. "Baby Hybrid . . . barrel roll!"

The hybrid launched into a desperate spin, climbing at the same time. The wings had to adjust just slightly to create the needed torque, but it was even more jarring than Lourdvang's barrel roll. Marcus barely held on, his fingers slipping against one another.

"Fire!" Dree shouted.

Baby Hybrid opened fire, scattering the drones and blowing part of the sheer canyon wall to rubble. They kept climbing for the surface, but the drones turned quickly, joining the other three. Marcus wondered how there could be more of them. He realized that the portal must have remained open—which meant there could be an endless number of drones arriving in Dracone if they didn't close it soon.

All five drones were firing now, and Dree had Baby Hybrid dancing across the sky, spinning and diving and twisting to avoid the constant barrage. They were just starting to pull away again when they saw two more drones approaching from the city.

"We're in trouble," Dree said.

Baby Hybrid veered left, avoiding another machine gun barrage, and just as the five drones were closing in, Marcus heard a terrible noise rise up from beneath them. Dree and Marcus both peered over the edge of the hybrid, and Dree's eyes widened.

"It can't be," she whispered.

There, streaming out of the canyon walls, were at least thirty golden dragons, glimmering in the dying light.

Chapter 24

The horde of Sages collided with the drones, ten of them converging on one and bathing it in a shimmering flame that leapt out like leaves from an autumn maple. The fire completely enveloped the Tracker and was followed soon after by a flurry of teeth and claws tearing into the armor and ripping the drone apart. Marcus knew immediately there would be no salvaging that drone: torn pieces—still fizzling electric blue—dropped into the river and disappeared.

For a moment he thought the dragons might wipe the drones out, but that hope was dashed the instant the drones wheeled around into a new formation—still four strong and bristling with weapons. They opened fire and downed one of the dragons in seconds.

The other Sages cried out in agony as they watched their companion plummet into the river, its wings nothing but tattered golden shreds. It was as if the other dragons felt the bullets themselves, and the cries filled Marcus and Dree with pain, so much so that they had to look away as the dragon hit the water. When the dragons attacked the drones again, it was with an even more terrible rage.

"We need to help," Dree said. "Baby Hybrid . . . turn around and fire!"

Baby Hybrid did as it was told, and the phalanx of drones scattered again, zooming in all directions through the enormous cavern. The dragons broke into units as well: Five of them chased each drone, spraying fire and roaring ceaselessly as they wheeled after the faster drones. Dree was absolutely astounded to see so many Sages still alive, and this close to the city. It seemed the Gully was their last great refuge, since the hunters could never pull a carcass from its deep walls. But even more surprising was the Sages' ferocity. Dree had heard that they were pacifists. Some legends even said they couldn't breathe fire.

Obviously they made an exception for the drones.

Dree kept Baby Hybrid racing after one Tracker in particular, firing constantly. Marcus barely held on to her waist as they dove and corkscrewed after the drone, shredding the cliff walls and covering the air with clouds of dust. They heard more terrible screams and saw two dead dragons drop into the river, sending up massive waves that lapped up over the shores. The air was full of hideous, anguished cries.

Marcus wanted to cover his ears, but he had to keep his arms wrapped around Dree.

"Dive!" Dree shouted, sending them angling toward the river. "Fire!"

The drone easily dodged the machine gun fire—Baby Hybrid was still too slow to respond to verbal commands. Meanwhile Sages were starting to fall everywhere, the drones moving too quickly for them to sink their claws and teeth into. Their fire was impressive, but it wasn't enough to down the armor-plated drones, and their guns were merciless. One dragon after another fell to its death.

Dree slammed her fist on the steel. "We're losing. Baby Hybrid, turn—"

"Wait," Marcus cut in. "We need to try something else."

"What do you mean?"

They both ducked as a drone whizzed overhead, dragons close behind.

"Do you tell Lourdvang how to fly?"

Dree turned and scowled. "Of course not."

"Then stop telling her," Marcus said. "Baby Hybrid . . . destroy the drones!"

Baby Hybrid immediately veered left, even before Dree saw the Tracker coming at them from above. The drone streaked past, and Baby Hybrid swept into a loop, causing both Dree and Marcus to scream as the distant canyon floor raced over their heads. They were still busy screaming when Baby Hybrid opened fire, hitting the drone's left wing as it tried to climb again. The bullets ripped into the metal, tearing it clean off. The drone wobbled and then flew straight into the side of the cliff, exploding in a massive fireball.

The dragons roared their approval and continued pursuing the remaining three drones.

Dree looked at Marcus. "Did you see that?"

"Yeah," he whispered.

Baby Hybrid turned after another Tracker, still slow to change directions but capable of incredible acceleration. The drone climbed skyward, and Baby Hybrid pursued it, clearing the flock of chasing golden dragons and closing in fast.

"We should have been doing this all along—" Marcus started.

He didn't get a chance to finish. The drone suddenly veered right, trying to escape, and Baby Hybrid followed in the fastest way possible—a quick barrel roll. Marcus wasn't ready. The g-forces ripped his hands from Dree's waist and sent him flying off of Baby Hybrid's back, his arms flailing desperately as he dropped out of the sky. Dree screamed and tried to grab his arm, but she was too late.

It was strange sensation, falling backward as the cold wind buffeted him while dragons and drones raced across the sky shooting bullets and flames at one another. It was so surreal that Marcus almost forgot to be scared, though he knew he was about a mile up and falling fast. He wouldn't even know when he hit the ground. Maybe that was better.

He saw Dree turning Baby Hybrid overhead, but she was already so far away. A drone raced past his head in a flash. Suddenly, something strong caught his shirt, instantly yanking him upward. He shouted and looked up to see beautiful golden scales glistening in the sun. One of the dragons had caught him.

"Hang on!" it rumbled, turning with its companions to chase the drones.

Marcus looked around and saw nothing to hold on to, so he just hugged himself.

Around them, the remaining three drones were still gunning down dragons. The Destroyer was particularly deadly: its machine guns were more powerful and its armor plating seemed almost impervious to the dragons' claws. At least ten of them had been killed already. Dree saw Marcus dangling from one of the dragon's legs and sent Baby Hybrid after one of the drones instead, relieved. For a second she had thought she'd lost him.

"Baby Hybrid," she ordered. "Dive and then loop, firing as you do."

Dree was playing a hunch now—the drones seemed to be paying a lot more attention to the hybrid after it had gunned down one of their own. She was counting on it.

Baby Hybrid launched into a dramatic dive, heading straight toward the river. Dree felt her legs slipping off the hybrid and held on tightly. The river grew ever larger.

"Now!" she screamed.

Baby Hybrid suddenly turned into a sharp loop, firing both guns. Her hunch paid off: They caught the Tracker on their tail head-on, and it exploded as the bullets pierced right through its blazing red eye. Baby Hybrid flew through the explosion, and Dree felt the flames stream past. If she hadn't been immune to them, she would have been dead.

The remaining two drones seemed to slow down for a moment, as if surveying the damage and their odds of victory. Marcus decided to use the advantage. As the dragon holding him flew over one of the drones, preparing to dive, Marcus looked up.

"Drop me!" he shouted.

"What?"

"Do it!"

The dragon snorted and let go, and Marcus dropped ten feet onto the back of the Destroyer, fumbling and grabbing onto the white steel plating. He pulled himself forward, looking for an access panel. The wind was screaming past him as the drone picked up speed again, firing on a group of dragons. One of them went down, crying out as it fell.

He had to hurry. Marcus spotted an access plate and popped it open, his eyes falling on an array of computer boards, wires, and switches.

He reached out to rip the wires when the drone veered up, almost pitching him off its back. It began to spin, and he felt his legs flying out as he just barely held on to the access panel, slipping ever so slightly. The world spun around him in a dizzying blur.

"Hold . . . still," he managed, reaching for the wires.

The drone finally turned again to fire on a dragon, and that gave Marcus the chance he needed. He ripped the wires and circuit board clean out, shorting the drone instantly. Marcus realized the problem with his plan just as the drone started to fall.

"Not again," he whispered.

The huge Destroyer dropped fast, speeding toward the canyon floor. Marcus let go instantly, floating off and trying to make himself big.

"Anyone?" he shouted, looking around desperately.

The dragons were forming together way above him, watching as the last drone suddenly took off out of the canyon, obviously retreating for the moment.

The ground was approaching fast.

"Are you ever not falling?" a familiar voice called, and he turned to see Dree racing down beside him, grinning and reaching out for his arm. He grabbed her hand, and she pulled him in as Baby Hybrid did a graceful curve upward, heading for the dragons.

"Thanks," he said.

"Don't mention it," she replied. "I owed you one anyway."

"The drones retreated, I see."

"Right after you took yours out. That was really dumb, by the way."

Marcus laughed. "I agree."

They slowed down in front of the group of dragons, and one of them gestured toward the canyon ledge. They all set down there, with many of the Sages inspecting one another's injuries. Almost all of them had holes in their wings or bloody wounds. But as Marcus and Dree watched, they began to heal each other with gentle, rippling copper flames that seemed to weld the scales and wings back together.

"Greetings," a male dragon said. "So you've found us."

Dree flushed. "And led the drones right to you."

The dragon shook his head. "They would have found us eventually. They kill every other dragon, and we knew it wouldn't be long before they found our home. Two of our kind were already killed as they hunted for deer. We wanted our vengeance. For machines, there is no mercy. After all, they give none."

Marcus looked up at the Sage, whose eyes were a tired opal and blue, his body smaller than Lourdvang's but still muscled. His scales had obviously been weathered by many years and looked as faded as Marcus's watch. But even as Marcus stared up at the dragon, he felt a sense of peace flood through him. Instantly his fears and anxiety ebbed.

"Is this all that's left of your kind?" Dree asked, looking over the group of dragons.

"I do not know," he said sadly. "There may be Sages elsewhere. But of my clan, once a hundred and fifty strong, there are now these eighteen of us. In time I fear there shall be none, even with this new weapon you ride upon."

"What's your name?" Dree asked.

The dragon looked at her. "Nolong. Why?"

Dree smiled. "Vero says hello."

Nolong's blue eyes widened. "You spoke with Vero?"

"She was hoping you were still alive."

Nolong looked to the east, frowning. "It has been many years since I last saw her."

"We know," Marcus said. "But she thinks of you anyway."

"It is nice to know she has not forgotten. Alas, such

concerns are far from my mind. For the moment, I must figure out how to keep my clan alive."

"There's only one chance," Dree said. "We're going after the Egg right now, but Erdath is also attempting to rally all the dragon clans together."

Nolong sighed. "A difficult task. Maybe impossible."

"It's also our only chance to defeat the drones," Marcus said. "You can be sure they'll have reinforcements."

Nolong seemed to consider this. "If we have one skill, it's speaking to other brethren. I will travel to all the clans I know and try to convince them to help. Perhaps I can rally them together. We have hid in this gully for long enough, letting our brothers and sisters die at the hands of dragon hunters and now these machines. It is time to fight back."

He looked at them both.

"There is something in the two of you," he said thoughtfully. "A power that I have not seen in many years. I do not know what it is, but do not be afraid to let it grow. I suspect you two will have a large part to play in this war, and it may not be the one you think."

He turned and left them, returning to his clan. Marcus tried to make sense of Nolong's words.

He turned to Dree, who looked equally puzzled.

"What now?" Marcus asked.

"We go break into the most heavily fortified place in Dracone and steal a priceless artifact."

Marcus sighed. "Perfect."

Chapter 25

Baby Hybrid descended onto the side of their chosen mountain, settling in an alcove covered with scraggly trees and shrubs. It overlooked the city below, which was lit with thousands of torches like lightning bugs in the plains. Dracone was quite beautiful from up there—bright and welcoming. But Dree knew it was also crawling with soldiers, and it was going to be very difficult to get into the palace, never mind to get out again.

Marcus's mind was elsewhere. He was finally returning to the city, and he was increasingly convinced that he would find his father somewhere within it. He didn't know what his father's part in all this was, but he knew the clues to his disappearance were everywhere. All Marcus could think about was seeing his father again. Of bringing him home.

Did Marcus even want to go home, though? He stole a glance at Dree, lit only by the faint moonlight shimmering off the mountain. He thought about her, and about what it felt like to ride on the back of a dragon. Did he really want to go back to Arlington?

One thing at a time, he told himself. First he had to try not to get arrested . . . or worse. He knew the soldiers wouldn't be kind to them following the prison break.

"Baby Hybrid," he said. "Fly away if anyone but us approaches and go back to Lourdvang at the den. But if I call, come straight to us. Try not to kill anyone."

Dree snorted. "What do you want her to do? Bring them flowers?"

"If it helps," Marcus said, patting the hybrid's wing. He was getting fond of her, lifeless though she was. Her eyes, locked on the city, blazed a fiery orange.

"Do you guys want a moment?" Dree asked.

"Shut up."

They started down the slope, being careful to avoid protruding rocks and crevices and any number of other hazards on the way. Marcus still stumbled on three separate occasions, twice relying on Dree to catch him and once face-planting on some shrubs. Scowling, he was still wiping the stinging thistles off of his face as they reached the bottom.

"We probably could have parked a little closer," he muttered.

"And risk being spotted?" Dree asked. "You're just not very graceful."

"Thanks."

She smiled. "Any time."

Dree led them into the untouched city, cutting through the ruined edges. The destruction was almost in a perfect ring, and as they passed into the downtown area, it looked like they were walking into the city exactly as it had been before the attacks. People were still out and about, lit by torchlight, and even the taverns were full. Dree saw a group of wealthy Draconians laughing and talking in front of a shop. Did these people not see what was happening around them? Didn't they care?

Dree felt her skin prickling and quickly looked away. An incident would not help them right now. But as they hurried toward the palace, her suspicions of the Prime Minister only grew. It looked like there wasn't a single bullet hole in the streets near the palace. The buildings were pristine. The merchant stands were still set up on the side of the road. Perhaps things had been chaotic, but they were already settling down. The attacks had stopped, and the city would slowly grow, sweeping the ruins aside like dirt. She thought of her family's home—nothing but wood and ash.

Could Francis really have had a part in this?

"There it is," Marcus whispered, as the palace came into view.

Torches lined its huge twenty-foot walls, flickering in the night. Soldiers stood at the barred entrance and on patrol around the perimeter, armed with swords and spears and bows. They could see at least thirty soldiers even from there—an impassable force.

"Where are these sewers?" Marcus asked nervously.

"They flow out toward the east end," she said. "There's a man-made trench there that goes out to a river in the mountains. Not pleasant, trust me."

"I can't wait."

They hurried through the city, trying to stay out of view of the soldiers. The night air smelled of warm fires on the hearth, stewed pork, and, slightly fainter, something much worse. Something bad. It grew stronger as they headed east, circling the palace. The shops became dingier again, and Marcus saw many refugees huddled together in the streets, gathered around small fires and cooking what looked disturbingly like rats.

"I guess this is where they sent the villagers," Dree said, her voice thick with contempt.

Soon the stench became stronger: sewage. Marcus felt his stomach turn at the prospect of climbing through anything making that kind of smell, but thankfully, Dree had a different plan in mind.

"That's our door," she said, pointing at another trench flowing *into* the palace.

That trench was filled with river water, obviously being diverted out of the mountains. It was only about ten feet away from the one leaving the palace—the source of the stench.

"Whew," Marcus said.

"Yeah," Dree said, grimacing. "Let's go."

They followed the trench to the castle wall, both of them looking for soldiers, though it seemed they didn't bother guarding the water and sewage systems, relying instead on the iron gates. Marcus and Dree huddled against the stone wall for a moment and then climbed down into the trench, the freezing water flowing right up to their waists. Marcus tried not to gasp. They both shivered as they moved with the strong current toward the gate. Dree kept her pack over the water, trembling violently.

"It's . . . so . . . cold," Marcus said.

"It's better than sewage," Dree retorted, removing her torch from the pack.

Marcus paused. "Agreed."

They stopped at the gate, where Dree put her torch to the iron, softening each joint. Marcus anxiously kept a watch behind them, knowing they were trapped if anyone spotted them. They would never make it out of the tunnel in time.

"Hurry," he said tersely.

"Working on it," she replied.

The torch was incredibly bright as it softened the iron joints, and finally, when they had melted enough, Dree took out her black hammer and pushed on them, welding at the same time. The softened iron folded inward. She did this to each joint, until a small opening was cut in the gate.

"Let's go," she said, heading through.

They moved quickly with the strong current, letting it carry them in. It was extremely dark in the tunnel, and

Marcus was just starting to feel a little claustrophobic when they finally saw flickering torchlight in front of them. They stayed close to the tunnel walls as they walked, keeping an eye out for movement. There was a large, old-fashioned wheel ahead, moving the water into aqueducts and sending it streaming through the castle. The wheel was sloshing the cold water around, creating a lot of noise, and they snuck up behind it onto a slimy concrete ledge built to service the wheel. There was a torch slung on the wall there, illuminating the bricks and the many cracks and crevices that ran through the tunnel. Marcus saw small eyes reflecting the light in the darkness. The whole area was crawling with rats.

"Stairs?" he suggested.

"Yes," Dree said.

It didn't take long. They found a set of slick concrete steps that led up out of the tunnel, the entire area smelling of mildew and mold. Marcus followed Dree up to a door at the top of the staircase, warm light spilling beneath it. Dree stopped there, listening.

Nothing.

She nodded at Marcus and eased the door open, cringing as the rusted hinges squeaked. They were in a hallway—clearly in a less-used area of the palace. The faded green walls were mostly bare aside from a few ancient paintings, and the floor was covered with a hideous beige carpet stained almost brown. Dree was amazed that any part of the palace would be allowed to fall into such disrepair, considering Francis had plenty of staff. They started down the hallway, looking from door to door.

"Where would the Egg even be?" Marcus asked, his eyes on a dusty portrait of an old man who seemed to be watching them. Marcus shuddered and looked away.

"How am I supposed to know?" she said. "I've never been here either."

"So we're going to look through the entire palace? What if the Egg's in the Prime Minister's bedroom or something?"

"Then we're in trouble," Dree said. "So let's hope it's not."

The hallway was lined with doors, but they all led to empty pantries and rundown storerooms and dusty wine cellars, tucked away in the damp and cold. The whole floor seemed abandoned. Finally they came to a broad staircase that led up to a pair of large, ornate wooden doors. Dree suspected the doors led to the main areas of the palace, which were sure to be filled with servants and soldiers. This was about to get tricky.

"Stay close," Dree whispered. "We need to be quiet."

Dree started up the staircase, crouching low. She turned back and saw Marcus still standing at the bottom of the steps, his eyes locked on something farther down the hall.

"What is it?" she whispered.

"Light," he replied, heading down the hallway.

Dree scowled and started after him. "What are you . . . a moth?"

Marcus shook his head, pointing. "Not torchlight. Blue light."

Dree followed his gaze and saw a door at the other end of the hall—a rotting wooden door like all the rest. But beneath it,

252

a strip of eerie blue light was shining through the small crack. She frowned. She had never seen light like that, apart from Marcus's laptop. It wasn't a light that belonged in Dracone.

"What is it?" she asked.

"I don't know," he said. "But I don't think it's another storage room."

They crept down the hall and stopped in front of the large padlocked door. Marcus glanced at Dree.

"Yeah, yeah," she said, pulling the pick out of her bag.

Within a minute, she had popped the lock off the door and then stood back.

"After you," Dree said.

Marcus pulled the door open, letting the blue light spill out into the hallway. He blinked against the sudden glare and saw another set of rough concrete stairs leading downward.

With one last glance in Dree's direction, Marcus started down the steps. He descended reluctantly, afraid of what he would find. . . . And when he finally reached the bottom of the concrete steps, he felt his knees buckle.

The ancient stone walls shimmered with an electric blue, as if they were in the midst of a lightning storm. The air was warm and dry, thrumming with the heat of hundreds of machines. It was like a living spiderweb of computer screens, power lines, and massive generators, all of them intertwined in an intricate pattern.

And there, sitting in the midst of the spiderweb, was George Brimley.

Chapter 26

"It can't be," Marcus whispered. But there was no doubting it was his father . . . or at least something that used to be his father.

His eyes were sunken and opaque, flicking across a row of screens flooded with numbers. His skin was pale and glowing the same luminescent blue as the machines, while his arms and legs were rope-thin and flaccid, propped up on a metal chair with unforgiving iron cuffs connected to his wrists and ankles. His hair was greasy and limp, falling over gaunt cheekbones like grasping vines that merged into a long, knotted chestnut beard. He was almost hidden behind the mess of hair, like a skeleton with a moth-eaten wig.

Dree saw the recognition on Marcus's face and put her

hand over her mouth in horror. That was the father he had been trying so desperately to find? She went to reach out for Marcus's shoulder, but he immediately stormed toward the web of machinery, heading straight for his father. He ducked under wires and power cells, his eyes welling.

He reached the chair, fully expecting his father to not even recognize him—to keep his eyes on the screens and continue on like the machine he seemed to have become.

But the second Marcus stepped in front of the chair, his father's cloudy blue eyes flicked to him and widened. The wrinkles on his face pulled tight with the shadow of a smile. He knew Marcus. His fingers moved, as if he was trying to reach out for him.

Marcus felt a flood of emotions: relief, despair, hope. He had been waiting for this moment for eight years, and to finally see his father now, like this, was almost too much to bear. But his father was in there, somewhere, and Marcus would save him.

"Marcus?" George said, his voice a hoarse croak. "Look at you. All grown up."

Marcus felt Dree step up beside him as tears started to roll down his face, but he didn't care. "I've come to bring you home," he said, looking at the screens. They showed pictures of automated assembly lines—conveyor belts running through some windowless factory. There were many different images, but he thought he saw wings and guns. "What is this?"

George's smile disappeared, sinking back into wrinkles

and ghostly skin. His lips were white and thin, as if they were of no use to him anymore and had died. "This is my folly."

Marcus, who was inspecting the cuffs to see if they could be ripped off, looked up at him and frowned. "What?"

Dree was examining the machinery, amazed that all of this existed in the bowels of the centuries-old palace. She ran her hands along a black wire, feeling the energy inside.

George nodded at the screens. "I built my own prison, I'm afraid." He glanced at Marcus, and now his clouded eyes were watering. "I thought I could make things better."

Marcus knelt down in front of him. "I don't understand. I thought . . . I thought you came here to close the portal. To stop the government from harvesting Dracone and killing everyone. Why else would the CIA call you a traitor?"

"Because I am one," George said simply.

Marcus stood up, trying to make sense of this. He had spent so much time convincing himself that his father was a victim—anything else seemed impossible. "A traitor to whom?"

"Myself," he said. "I stole something from the CIA. Something very valuable. The plans for those drones . . . many years ago. I took them here, where I knew they could never find me. I have many secrets, Marcus. And for you, they will not be easy to hear."

"Maybe we should get you out of here," Dree suggested uneasily.

"No," George said. "Marcus deserves to know the truth first." He paused. "In case he wants to leave me here with my many mistakes."

"What truth?" Marcus asked.

George met his eyes. "I was not born in the United States, Marcus. I was born and raised in a town just outside of this city. I was a loner growing up, more interested in machinery than games. It was my only passion. Well, that and a girl named Lenda Faller, who lived two houses over." He smiled, but it was pained. "She wasn't interested in me, of course—she was of a wealthy family—but I pursued her anyway, and one day, when we were seventeen, she finally agreed to a date. We were married two years later in a beautiful ceremony in town."

His eyes glazed over even more, as if he was looking at something long ago. Dree glanced at Marcus, some pieces falling into place. He had Draconian blood in his veins.

"Was that . . . Mom?" Marcus asked.

"Yes. I loved her dearly," George whispered. "And then I killed her."

George tried to reach out to take Marcus's hand, but he pulled it away.

"What do you mean?" Marcus said.

George sighed. "I was vain. Your mother was a dragon rider, one of the best. She had a dragon named Sera, a Sage. When you were born, I knew immediately that you had her blood. You would be a rider too. I wanted to become one as well."

His sunken eyes flicked to Marcus.

"I was already the leading engineer in Dracone. I was close with Francis Xidorne, and when he came to power, he let me work on new projects. There was one I kept from him, though. A mechanical dragon . . . a mount for a rider who would never be chosen."

Dree and Marcus exchanged a knowing look.

"I was successful enough," George said, "but it wasn't quite right. It would never match a real dragon. And so I set off for the one thing that would help."

"The Egg," Dree whispered.

George nodded. "I stole it and brought it back to my town. I was going to use it."

"You're from Toloth," Dree said. It wasn't a question.

"Yes," George whispered. "Helvath came out of the mountain that night, along with two other Flames. They destroyed my town and killed everyone in it. My wife tried to fight them with Sera, but they were both slain. The only survivors were Marcus and me."

Marcus frowned. "But how did you . . . we . . . end up in the other world?"

"I was lost without Lenda," George said. "I sat with you in the smoking ruins, wondering how I would protect you if the Flames returned. We were powerless against such creatures, and they had a vendetta against me. At any moment, they might return for my only son . . . the only thing of value I had left. A year earlier I had started a new project, spatial distortions. Even then I believed that a land existed parallel to Dracone, and that it could only be accessed with energy."

"The storms," Marcus said softly.

"Precisely. By creating energy disruptions I found a

way to open a portal, and we used it to escape. I started a new life in the new world, taking a job with the CIA and raising you. But as the years passed, my guilt grew for what I had done. I decided to go back and help Francis safeguard our people against the Flames and build a better world. I stole the drone technology I had been working on, and I asked Jack to watch you so I could return to Dracone."

Dree looked at him, frowning. "You worked on the drones?"

"I helped design them," he said. "I built the first ones here five years ago." He paused. "I tried to leave you clues. The symbol . . . I had hoped it would lead you to me."

"The symbol on the drones?" Marcus asked.

"Yes. The three rectangles. The place we always wanted to go."

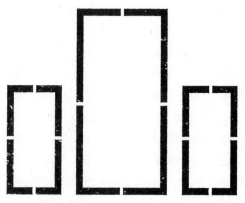

"Oz," Marcus whispered. "The towers. That's what you wrote on your desk."

"Yes," he said.

Marcus shook his head. "But it wasn't just the towers on

the drone wings. There were two eyes above them as well."

"Eyes?" George asked. He sighed. "Of course. Those must have been added later."

Marcus sat down on the stone floor, his mind reeling. He felt like he might be sick. Dree knelt down beside him, rubbing his back. Her eyes were locked on George, disturbed. Who was this man? Why would he build machines that killed innocent people?

"What happened?" Marcus whispered.

George looked away. "I put my trust in the wrong person. Francis changed over the years. He wanted more and more power—not just to defend against the Flames, but to destroy all of the dragons. To destroy the revolutionaries. To destroy anyone who didn't agree with him. He wanted to become an emperor."

George let out a defeated sigh.

"He asked me to adjust the drones' programming. I agreed, but I stalled, knowing that he would only use them for evil. As the years passed, he realized what I was doing. A year ago he decided to imprison me here and take over the drone program himself. He must have added those eyes. . . . He was always watching me, and I guess he wanted to prove it. In my desperation, I sent the last few drones I still controlled into your world to find you, to keep you safe and bring you back to Dracone. I succeeded, but now Francis has full control over them too, and I fear he will use them to destroy anything in Dracone that threatens him . . . the dragons, the poor, and all who would dare to stand against him."

George glanced at Marcus.

"He just needs one more thing to make the drones invincible. The Egg. It's an energy source: It emanates the same fiery energy that the dragons have within them. It has the ability to endow robotics with life—to turn them into something nearly invincible. But when I realized the danger it posed, I decided to hide it back on Earth. I returned, hid the Egg, and then came back to Dracone to try and fix my mistakes. But I was too late."

"Why?" Marcus asked, almost angrily.

"For the same reason I hid the Egg. I had been betrayed." He looked at Marcus, and for the first time, there was fear in his eyes. "And when I returned, he put me here."

"Yes," a quiet voice said.

Marcus and Dree turned to see Francis Xidorne walking out of the shadows, the friendly smile he always wore twisted into something dark and cruel. His eyes fell on George, who had shrunken into his chair, terrified.

"And I want that Egg."

Chapter 27

Marcus and Dree took a step backward, unnerved by the sardonic expression on Francis's face. When Dree had seen him last, he looked jovial and warm—now he looked malicious. Merciless.

Francis watched them for a moment, his hands clasped behind his back.

"Your father was quite right about the rest of it. We worked together to do two very simple things: destroy the dragons and create a better Dracone. When I realized he was abandoning these goals—his weakness had caused him to feel remorse for those flying worms—it became clear that our visions for the future of this world didn't quite align. He was going to throw it all away. I couldn't allow that, of course, so I acted."

Marcus looked at his father. "Why didn't you stop him?"

"He commands the Protectorate," George said. "He is far too powerful here. He locked me in this room to watch his work and took over the control of the drones. As I sat here, he began to build his army. Beneath that steel mill is a factory. They're building drones."

"You're making more of them?" Dree whispered.

George nodded. "Many more."

"But too slowly," Francis said. "I wanted improvements in the manufacturing process, but your father refused to help me. To make matters worse, he managed to send some of the drones I did have to your world in an attempt to have them shot down and destroyed. Thankfully you brought them back for me."

He smiled coolly.

"They are now firmly in my control. I have since been using the drones to destroy the poorer outskirts and remove some . . . unfortunate elements of society."

"The revolutionaries," Dree whispered.

"Yes. And their miserable families. A breeding ground for rebellion. Once Dracone is cleared, I can fully turn my attention to the worms. The Outliers have been simple to take down, and the Nightwings will be next. But even I wonder if the drones can destroy the Flames."

He turned to George.

"And so I asked him for the Egg, but he insisted it was gone. Now I know he was lying. I will need you to go retrieve it for me, George."

Marcus climbed to his feet, looking at Francis in disgust. "He won't do anything of the sort." He turned and started fiddling with the steel cuffs. "We're out of here."

Francis smiled, flashing his ivory teeth. "Marcus and George can go. Driele Reiter, you'll stay here with me to make sure they return with the Egg. If they don't, I will kill you and your family. Even little Abigale."

"How do you know my name?" Dree asked quietly.

He laughed. "You don't think I stopped watching my old friend Abelard, do you? He was always against me, your father. He loved the old ways. But I made sure to get him out of my way early on."

"What did you do?" Dree whispered.

"After I ended the days of the dragon riders, your father grew restless," Francis said. "He was onto my plans. But he was too careless. He started organizing rallies, leading the underground, talking of revolution. I could have had him killed, but that wasn't enough for such insolence. You do not defy this government—you do not defy *me*—without facing consequences. I wanted him broken. You may not know this, but I own those dockyards. He worked for me."

Francis met Dree's eyes, a smirk on his face once again.

"Well, one day your father's coworkers didn't show up on my orders. We still needed the boat stocked with very heavy steel supplies. Crates upon crates of them. He struggled, asking for help, but the dockmaster told him he would be fired if he left. He knew it was me, and so he struggled on. He thought he could show that he was stronger than me, that he would never give up. But the day wore on, he tired, and eventually, near the end, he broke."

Francis leaned in a little.

"The dockmaster told me that when his back snapped, he cried out for his dragon. We let him lie there for hours, writhing in pain, knowing that he had lost everything."

Dree bolted toward Francis, balling her fists. She'd felt the heat building, and now he'd pushed her too far. She swung right for his face, thinking how good it was going to feel to knock him into the next room. She heard Marcus's father shouting something behind her, but she ignored him. She'd had enough talk.

Francis reacted almost instantly.

Still smiling, he lifted a small weapon and pulled the trigger. An electric blast collided with Dree's stomach, enveloping her entire body. The effect was devastating.

Energy flooded through her like a blast of lightning, sending her flying across the room and smashing into the hard concrete wall twenty feet away. Her right shoulder crunched painfully under the blow, and she dropped to the cold floor, dazed and shaking.

"Dree!" Marcus shouted, starting toward Francis.

"No!" George said firmly. "I was trying to warn her. I designed that weapon . . . he stole it from me a year ago."

Dree groggily tried to stand, feeling weak. She looked at Francis, seething. The heat was coursing through her like lava, but she couldn't find the strength to get up again.

"Take him out," she managed.

Francis sighed. "I think not." He took a small metallic transmitter out of his pocket and pressed it. "Activate."

Suddenly, dual red lights lit up in the darkness behind Xidorne. Two Trackers slowly glided forward. They must have been parked at the back of the cavernous dungeon behind some of the excess machinery. Their machine guns were at the ready. Dree froze.

"Marcus," Francis said quietly, "you will take your father back to Arlington. You will retrieve the Egg and you will bring it back to me. If you don't, I will kill Dree and every other living person in this city. I don't really *need* them, you see. Do you understand?"

"What will you do if you have the Egg?" Marcus asked.

"Kill the dragons. All of them. Purge the countryside. Build a better Dracone."

Francis smiled.

"After all, that is the job I was elected for."

Marcus exchanged a quick glance with Dree and then slid his hand into his pocket, where his phone was tucked against his leg. Trying to remain inconspicuous, he slid his finger over the screen and opened the keypad—he knew the phone so well he didn't even need to see the screen to operate it. He pressed One and then Call, activating the homing beacon he had installed in Baby Hybrid.

The drones tilted slightly, one locked on Dree and the other on Marcus.

"Now," Francis said, "let's get this moving, shall we? Dree, you can take a seat in the corner. I suspect it will take these two some time. I know you can create the disruptions on demand, George, my old friend, though you refuse to admit it. I suggest you do it quickly."

Marcus removed the heavy metal cuffs from George's wrists and ankles, and he gasped when he saw the deep red bruises and callouses that had formed from being stuck in them for so long. George almost fell out of the chair, but Marcus grabbed him.

"I'm sorry, Marcus," he whispered. "I'm so sorry."

"It's okay, Dad," Marcus said, even though he wasn't sure he meant it. He wasn't sure what to think. But right now, they just had to get out of the palace.

"You and your father can catch up later," Francis said. "Move along."

Marcus hesitated, but Francis aimed the weapon at Dree again, and the two enormous Trackers floated ominously behind him, machine guns trained on Marcus and his father. He needed to waste time.

"All right," Marcus replied, "we're going."

Dree turned to Marcus, scowling. "We're not getting you that Egg. Right, Marcus?"

Marcus groaned inwardly. Could she not just pretend for a second? "Well . . ."

She narrowed her eyes, and he sighed. He couldn't stand her look of betrayal.

"No," Marcus said.

Francis gave another exaggerated sigh. "I see we might need a little motivation." He took the transmitter out again.

"Drone three, open fire on the west block of—"

"Wait," Marcus said quickly. "We'll go."

He ignored the look on Dree's face. He could deal with her disappointment for a little longer. He wasn't letting anyone else get killed.

"Wise choice. Dree, make yourself comfortable—"

He was cut off by a massive, wall-shaking boom. The dungeon ceiling flaked and shook, knocking Marcus and George to the unforgiving stone ground. Francis looked up.

"What was that?" he asked.

"You might want to duck," Marcus said to Dree, and she immediately hit the floor. She was just in time. Part of the dungeon ceiling blew open in a hail of bullets, shredding the ancient stones, and Baby Hybrid emerged through the smoke, streaking right through the decimated palace hallways. Behind her, half the palace had been blown open, revealing the night sky. Dust and ash swirled everywhere, and Marcus spotted Francis crawling away from the rubble.

He turned to the drones. "Shoot it down!"

The Trackers wheeled toward Baby Hybrid, opening fire, and the hybrid took off for the sky again, leading them away. The drones screamed after it.

"I can't believe it," George said, watching Baby Hybrid soar out of the palace. "It's better than the one I made. It's . . . beautiful."

"Dree did most of it," Marcus replied, wiping the dust from his eyes. "Dree, you okay?"

"Fine," she managed. "Baby Hybrid might be a bit *too* eager with her rescues, though."

Five heavily armed soldiers appeared in one of the shattered hallways overhead—three stories had been torn open in the attack—looking completely bewildered when they saw the electric blue machinery. They spotted Francis and shouted for orders.

Francis pointed at Marcus and George. "Intruders in the palace," he screamed. "Seize them all immediately and bring them to the prisons."

The first soldier lowered himself from the upper floor hallway and dropped to the ground, ready to charge Marcus. He didn't see Dree slowly pushing herself up in the darkness behind him. She lashed out with a sharp kick to the back of his leg, crumpling him, and then struck him across the chin, knocking him out. She scooped up his broadsword and tossed a small knife to Marcus, letting it fall short and slide toward his feet.

"Take out Francis!"

Marcus scooped up the knife, leaving George to lean heavily on the chair. He charged Francis as two more soldiers dropped down to face a now sword-wielding Dree. But Francis was faster. He hurried toward the staircase, shouting for more soldiers.

Dree waved her sword around wildly, keeping the two soldiers at bay, but when the remaining two dropped down, she knew she was in trouble. They were just advancing toward her when Baby Hybrid swept over the room, spraying machine gun fire and downing two of the soldiers. The remaining two soldiers scattered for cover, and Francis was forced to dive out of the way as the entrance to the staircase was torn apart. The doorway collapsed into a heap of rubble, trapping them all inside. Baby Hybrid slowed down for just a moment to survey the room, searching for Dree and Marcus, and one of the drones used the delay to fire on its right wing, tearing some of the armor away. Baby Hybrid buckled under the fire and then shot skyward again out of the decimated palace.

Marcus closed in on Francis, the knife shaking in his hands. He had never used a weapon before, but he had seen a lot of movies and kept it well in front of him, pointed at Francis's chest. Francis looked up as Marcus approached. He was still smiling.

Francis lifted the energy weapon and fired. The blast hit Marcus like a truck, and he flew backward and crashed onto the floor, the knife spilling from his hands. He heard his father cry out and try to get to him, and then a loud thud as his legs gave out.

The two soldiers were up again and attacking Dree, who was barely holding them off, waving her sword back and forth frantically from where she was pinned to a wall. She had wielded swords many times to test their weight and speed in the forge, but she had never actually fought anyone with them. It was exhilarating and terrifying and almost mindless—all she could think of was avoiding the steel death raining down on her from the two large, grizzled men in black armor. She jumped behind a computer screen and watched in satisfaction as one of the soldiers stabbed into it, shocking himself in a sizzle of blue and dropping his sword, cursing.

Overhead, Baby Hybrid was in trouble. Three more drones had joined the pursuit, including a Destroyer, and the hybrid was racing in and out of the palace hallways, trying to avoid the constant fire. Sparks burst out behind it like a comet's tail as bullets deflected off the heavy armor that Dree had worked for weeks to assemble. Another piece of its wing flaked away, and Dree saw a bullet hit the right engine, causing a short. Baby Hybrid wobbled but kept flying and even managed to blow one of the drones apart with a missile. The fireball raced through the palace hallways, engulfing plush carpets and statues and gold-framed pictures.

Marcus groaned and climbed back to his feet, his whole body tingling. As he stood up, he saw Francis walking toward him, the smile gone. He looked angry now.

"I begin to wonder if you are worth keeping alive," he said, looking at George thoughtfully. "But I need that Egg." He leaned down. "Pick up your father and get to the portal."

He stood up straight and pointed the weapon at Marcus's head.

"You won't survive a shot to the face, boy," he said quietly.

"We'll go," George said weakly, crawling toward Marcus. "Leave my son."

"Then hurry," Francis replied. "I am becoming impatient."

Across the room, Dree met swords with the final soldier.

She strained to push him back, but he was too strong. He suddenly twisted his blade, sending hers flying across the dungeon. Without warning, he backhanded her viciously and she toppled backward, dazed. Dree hit the ground and pain raced up her spine. She watched in numb defeat as the soldier stepped over her. His eyes locked on hers as he lifted the sword. It was over. She had failed, and she would die here in the bowels of the palace.

Dree looked up and saw Baby Hybrid take another flurry of gunfire, its right engine completely shorting out. It began to spin, losing power. It was going down.

Two of the drones left the pursuit and glided over the dungeon, their machine guns locked on her and Marcus. To make matters worse, another regiment of black-armored soldiers appeared in the hallways above them—at least thirty strong.

"It's over," Francis said. His eyes flicked to Dree. "The girl is an assassin. Kill her."

"No!" Marcus shouted. "You said—"

"I said I would keep her alive if you left," Francis replied. "You did not."

The soldier smiled and gripped the sword with two hands, preparing to bring it down. Dree had another image of Gavri, smiling at her. She knew she would see him soon. But strangely enough, she didn't want to now. She had so much more to do.

There was a glint of light as the sword fell.

It never made it. Suddenly, raging crimson fire burst across the exposed palace, flooding the upper hallway and scattering the soldiers. The man who was about to kill Dree was snatched up in long black talons and pitched across the room, while the two hovering Trackers were forced to veer away from the incredible force of the flames. Lourdvang roared as he turned back to Dree, his eyes blazing with rage, and she jumped to her feet and leapt onto his neck as soon as he landed.

Above them, where part of the palace had been blown open, the sky had filled with black and golden shapes as Sages and Nightwings converged on the drones. Dree spotted Nolong as he landed on one of the Destroyer's enormous white wings, trying to tear into the heavily reinforced armor. George stumbled toward the machinery and grabbed a small transmitter that was tucked into the shadows, jamming it into his pocket.

"Come on!" Dree shouted.

Marcus grabbed his father and started pulling him over to Lourdvang, but suddenly realized that his father couldn't touch Lourdvang without being burned.

"We need Baby Hybrid," he said. "Where is—"

He didn't get the chance to finish. They heard another explosion overhead and looked up to see a flaming Baby Hybrid streaking into the room, fire billowing out behind it. It hit the ground and skidded into the rows of blinking machinery, its forward engines both blown out. The hybrid rolled and landed on its side, revealing one of its machine guns, and it promptly started firing behind them, scattering the two Trackers.

"Hurry!" Dree screamed.

Marcus turned to his dad. "Get on my back."

"Just leave me—"

"No," Marcus said firmly. He wasn't losing his father again. "Get on."

He knelt down and George climbed onto his back. He was a tall man, but he was now so thin and frail that Marcus managed to stand up again, though his knees were shaking. He climbed up onto Lourdvang's back, George clinging to him weakly, his yellowed fingers interwined on Marcus's chest. Every step was a trial, and Marcus's body ached and strained and trembled, but he managed to pull himself up and sit behind Dree, gripping his father's legs beneath his arms. George was only inches from Lourdvang's blazing hot scales.

"Go!" Dree shouted.

Lourdvang leapt into the air, using the distraction to race through the hole blasted into the side of the palace and streak toward the stars. A horde of dragons was waiting there, covering their escape. Marcus turned back to see the remaining drones gather around Francis, who was slowly walking over to the hybrid. Even from there, Marcus could see his calculating smile. Francis knew that he still had his weapon.

"Should we go back?" Dree asked, following Marcus's gaze.

"No," Marcus said, struggling to hold on to his father's slender legs. "Let's just get out of here."

They flew away in silence, leaving the flaming, ruined palace behind them. Both Marcus and Dree felt sick for abandoning Baby Hybrid, like they were leaving a family member behind. Baby Hybrid may have been machine, but it had saved their lives yet again.

"He knows how to rebuild it, doesn't he?" Marcus asked his father, who was clutching Marcus's chest desperately, his sickly, flaccid arms barely holding on to him.

"Yes," George replied. "Without the Egg, we will have no chance of stopping him."

"So what do we do now?" Dree asked.

George paused. "We find the Egg first. And we get ready for war."

Marcus looked back as they sailed into the mountains, his eyes on the fires raging behind them. He thought of all the people that had been killed. All of the dragons.

Fire flooded through him, just waiting to erupt.

"We're ready," he said. "Let the war begin."

Chapter 28

Dree and Marcus stood alone on the exposed ledge outside the Nightwings' lair, watching the sun rise over the horizon. It lit the snow-covered mountains with golden fire, matching the clouds sweeping overhead. It was cold up on the summit, but the usually fierce wind was gentle for once, meandering through the valleys on its long way south.

No one had slept that night. They had spoken at great length with Erdath, who had managed to rally his own people for war. He had also sent envoys out to the other clans in Dracone, and when he heard that Nolong was going to try as well, he seemed relieved.

"My kin likely would not have succeeded," Erdath had said. "But a Sage is a different thing altogether." He'd looked out over his kin, concern in his green eyes. "If Francis can create more drones, then we will need even more dragons. I fear that to win we may need the most dangerous ones of all."

"They'll never help us," Lourdvang said.

"Then we must find a way to convince them," Erdath replied.

George had finally gone to sleep in the side caverns, using Marcus's backpack as a pillow. He had collapsed onto the ground almost instantly, clearly exhausted after months imprisoned in the dungeon.

Marcus still didn't know what to think about his father. He was of course overjoyed to see him again, but he was also appalled by the things he had done. George had stolen the Egg, gotten his mother killed, and lied to Marcus his entire life. Then he'd returned to Dracone and built the very drones that were now destroying the countryside and murdering thousands.

It was a sickening feeling to know that his father was partially to blame for these deaths.

But what was Marcus supposed to do? Turn his back on the only family he had left? He couldn't just abandon his father, regardless of what he had done. And his father did truly seem to want to make amends—in fact, he seemed obsessed with it.

They had spoken in the cavern before he slept.

"I'll create the disruption tomorrow," he said grimly, showing Marcus the transmitter that he had kept hidden for years. "I have sensor relays stationed around Dracone. When I signal, the storm will begin."

Marcus nodded. "And what about Francis?"

"He'll find a way to get them there," he said. "He's learning fast. We'll need to get the Egg, get back to Dracone, and see if we can rescue your Baby Hybrid or build another one." He took Marcus by the shoulder. "I'm going to make this right, son."

Marcus had just faked a smile. For some reason, it didn't feel right calling George his father yet. Maybe in time. But for now, he still had too many questions.

Dree was going to go with them to Earth as well. Despite George's insistence that he wanted to defeat Francis and return Dracone to the way it was before, she didn't trust him, and she definitely didn't want to leave him alone with Marcus.

"A lot has happened in a few weeks," Dree said quietly, watching the sunrise.

"Yeah," Marcus replied. "Everything . . . I think. I forget what my life was like before."

"Me too. And maybe that's a good thing for the two of us."

Marcus paused and looked at her, shifting a little. "Thank you."

"For what?" she asked.

"Saving my life a thousand times, for starters, but also for showing me all this . . . for showing me where I belong."

"Will you go back?" Dree asked softly. "You know . . . after?"

"What for?" he said. "My life is here now—this is my world—I was born in Dracone. And now I have to make up for what my father has done."

Dree felt her skin prickling. It was all she could do not to storm into the cavern and punch Marcus's father. He had launched the destruction of the dragons. He had helped Francis, who had given the orders to have her family stripped of its wealth. He had ruined so many lives. But what could she do? He was Marcus's father, and she didn't want to hurt Marcus. They could deal with his crimes when Francis and the drones were defeated.

The sun peaked over the mountains, chasing the last shadows away.

"What about your family?" Marcus asked.

"I'll leave them in the caves for now. It's safest there. Abi will miss me, but it's for the best. I won't go anywhere near there now. . . . Francis will have the drones searching everywhere for us."

"He's probably busy with Baby Hybrid," Marcus said.

"We'll get her back." Dree squeezed his hand. The heat warmed them both, racing up their arms.

"We have to," Marcus said. "If Francis has a working hybrid and an army of drones, we don't have much chance against him. Even with the Flames."

Dree shook her head. "We still need to actually try and recruit the Flames."

"I can't wait to go see Helvath again," Marcus muttered.

Dree laughed. "One thing at a time. Your world, first. Should we get your dad?"

"Yeah," he said, sighing. "We have a storm to catch."

✦

Marcus, George, and Dree climbed off of Lourdvang's back at the base of the southwestern valley, completely hidden by the mountains. Sweeping plains opened up just ahead, where the three humans would walk into the heart of the storm that was already raging in the distance and approaching fast. Marcus turned to Lourdvang and patted his nose.

"Thanks for everything," he said. "We'll be back soon."

"Make sure of it," Lourdvang grumbled.

Marcus smiled and turned away, letting him have a moment with Dree.

"You're sure I can't come with you?" Lourdvang asked.

Dree smiled. "From what I understand, you might be a bit conspicuous."

He snorted, shooting out a great puff of black smoke. "So?"

"We're trying to retrieve the Egg," she said. "That means a little bit of secrecy."

"I don't like it," he said simply. "What if you get into trouble over there?"

"We'll be fine."

"That's what you said before you stormed the palace," he pointed out.

Dree hesitated. "This time I mean it." She wrapped his massive neck in a hug, feeling the warmth against her cheek. "We'll be back as soon as possible. I promise."

"You better be," he muttered, eyeing George at the same time. "Watch him."

"I will," she said. "See you soon, little brother."

Waving goodbye, they started into the grassy plains, struggling against the fierce wind. Lightning was flashing across the sky, and they were about a half mile in when rain suddenly broke in a great sheet, soaking them all to the core. Dree laughed as the freezing cold rain beat down on her cheeks. She loved storms. Marcus was preoccupied though, searching for the heart of it—where the lightning was most intense. Finally, he pointed at a particularly dark cloud in the midst of the storm, and they hurried toward it, George still moving slowly.

Marcus looked at his father with concern. Despite a full night's sleep, he still looked very frail. The wind was nearly picking him up as it swept past them toward the mountains, grabbing at his filthy clothes and skeletal limbs.

"What are these disruptions anyway?" Marcus called over the wind.

"Spatial anomalies," George replied. "Disruptions in space-time, to be exact. Much as Stephen Hawking speculated with multiverses—I believe that Dracone and Earth exist in parallel universes. I placed a ring of temporal energy projectors around Dracone, and later around Arlington, to bring myself back. When I create energy at a certain frequency, it opens the rift. It only happens on one side and then sweeps through the other for just a moment when something disrupts the energy flow and is transported."

Another tremendous fork of lightning split the sky.

Dree watched it dance through the clouds and then froze. There were black and white spots in the sky overhead. Lots of them. She scanned the storm, spotting at least ten.

"Guys . . ."

"I see them," Marcus said. "Get to the center of the storm. Now!"

They all broke into a sprint, following Marcus across the sprawling meadow. The drones leapt into action, and a missile exploded into the ground nearby, sending up a massive plume of dirt and fire. The three of them kept running across the open plains as gunfire and missiles started to rain down from above, joining the barrage of bitterly cold rain. The drones swooped down in a diamond point, heading straight for them.

"Where is it?" Dree asked desperately, looking behind them.

"There!" Marcus shouted.

They raced beneath the most violent cloud, lit up by nearly constant blasts of lightning. The drones opened again, and machine gun fire chewed into the dirt, speeding toward them faster than they could possibly run.

Dree looked back, knowing that they would be torn apart in moments.

"Marcus—"

"Jump!" he screamed, watching as a massive bolt of lightning split the sky and raced downward.

Marcus leapt off the ground, Dree and his father close

behind, and he heard the machine guns close in just as a brilliant flash of blue lit up his vision. He felt himself falling, seeing nothing but light, and then he slammed hard into concrete, hearing groans as Dree and his father did the same thing behind him.

"Ow," Dree muttered, squinting against the glaring sunlight.

Dree and Marcus gingerly climbed to their feet, pulling George up with them, and then looked around.

They were in the middle of downtown Arlington in the morning rush hour, and a huge crowd of people were looking at them in utter shock, their hair windblown and their purses and coffee cups and newspapers scattered everywhere like misshapen hailstones. It was eerily silent for a long moment, and then whispers and conversations erupted everywhere as the crowd stared at the new arrivals.

Marcus slowly turned to Dree, smiling awkwardly. "Welcome to Earth."

Acknowledgments

I would like to start by thanking Ben Schrank at Razorbill for giving me this amazing opportunity. I love spending time with Marcus and Dree, and I can't wait to continue. Also thanks to my editor, Marissa Grossman, for helping me craft an engaging story and a world that readers will hopefully love. And thank you to the rest of the team at Razorbill for all your work putting this book together. I have felt right at home since we started.

As always, I would like to thank my wonderful agent, Brianne Johnson, who has been with me from the beginning and who will hopefully keep me around for a long time to come. Thank you as always for your insight, advice, and inspiration to tackle new projects.

Thank you to my loving wife, Juliana, who continues to bear with me while I journey off into worlds of dragons and sometimes forget to come home for dinner (which is still delicious when it gets reheated). To my always encouraging family, thank you for always being there to read anything and everything I throw your way. And because your older brother got to be in a book, welcome to the world, Dallas! Your brother may get to journey off to space, but you get to ride a dragon.

It seems for almost every book I write, someone I care about has passed away before it could come out, and this one was no different. We lost my beloved father-in-law, Rick Niedziela, after a long and incredibly arduous fight against cancer. He fought for every minute, as was his way, and when he finally left, he went on his own terms. We miss you greatly, and we will never forget the many, many things you taught us.

And finally, because he keeps getting skipped over, thanks to Paul N.